DUSK

DEATH ISLAND

JERVIS T.C.H.

PARTRIDGE
A Penguin Random House Company

Copyright © 2014 by Jervis T.C.H..

ISBN:	Hardcover	978-1-4828-2384-4
	Softcover	978-1-4828-2383-7
	eBook	978-1-4828-2385-1

To order additional copies of this book, contact
Toll Free 800 101 2657 (Singapore)
Toll Free 1 800 81 7340 (Malaysia)
orders.singapore@partridgepublishing.com

www.partridgepublishing.com/singapore

CONTENTS

ABOUT THE AUTHOR

Born in 1992, Jervis (pen name Jervis T.C.H.) is a Singaporean science fiction novelist who has written and published his first full length debut novel titled Dusk: Galactic Paradise in June 2012, and currently holds a Diploma in Environmental Science after graduating from Republic Polytechnic in 2013.

MESSAGE FROM
THE AUTHOR

Good day to all my readers! I would first of all like to thank all of you for showing interest in my work.

In the beginning, this work was only meant to be a short story of around 3,000 words, but it unexpectedly grew into a much larger work, and ended at around 23,600 words due to the continuous conception of ideas during writing and editing. Ultimately, it became a novella, which is longer than a short story but shorter than a full length novel.

Also, if you have the time, do leave a like at our Facebook page (Dusk: Death Island) at https://www.facebook.com/pages/Dusk-Death-Island/733966649980904 to show your support! Alternatively, you can also type the title of this novella into the search box to enter the page.

I would also like to thank and give credit to Mary Baldwin for providing me with the blue phoenix for the cover design.

Last but not least, enjoy this epic story! This is only the beginning!

HOW THIS NOVEL
SERIES STARTED

The author's interest in astronomy was sparked in 1999. Overtime, he became so passionate about it that he doesn't want to just know more about the universe, but also to literally explore it. Hence, he created an imaginary world within his mind in 2005 to satisfy this need—by creating his own personal ship and cooperation. This was also done to escape the hardships of reality.

Eventually, this imaginary world of his became so real that the amount of time taken for him to fly his ship from one star system to another is the same as the amount of time passed in real world time. Over the years, this imaginary world of his became so excessively developed due to inspirations from Harry Potter and the Halo series that it led to the creation of the Universe of Dusk that you see today.

STORY TIMELINE

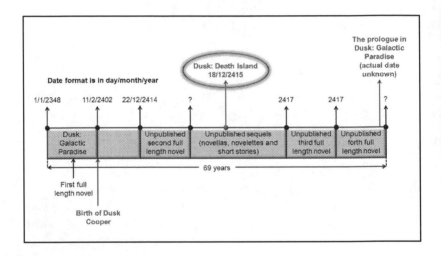

The following above displays the chronological timeline of this series. This novella took place after Dusk Cooper, Raven Emerson and Keegan Holman joined Rubicon, School of PDA Applications and Technologies in Telrux University after the events in the second full-length novel.

I began writing this novella on November 11, 2013, and finished on April 18, 2014. Editing pushed all the way till June 2014 for production.

THIS NOVELLA BELONGS
TO HEXIRON MEMBER

_____

Race: Human / Scentellian / Human-Scentellian

PRESENTED FROM

_____

Race: Human / Scentellian / Human-Scentellian

ON PLANET

_____

CHAPTER 1

THE ARRIVAL

December 18, 2415

In a star system far in the Milky Way Galaxy, three good friends, Dusk, Keegan, and Raven, were on an expedition of planetary exploration in a small frigate known as the *Heron*.

At the age of thirteen, Dusk was short and thin, and being a half-human and half-Scentellian, his skin was partially covered in hard, yellow scales, similar to those on snakes. However, he also had certain physical characteristics that resembled ordinary human beings, such as smooth, peach-colored skin, as well as black hair.

They were flying high above the surface of an extraterrestrial Earth-like planet called Amiros, greatly enjoying its scenic geographical landscapes (primarily oceans and islands) and even some of the largest wildlife it harbors. Its skies high above were also decorated with magnificent, brightly lit ring systems that were as broad as a quarter of its diameter. It appeared whitish in color and comprised millions of smaller ringlets, rendering it a splendid icon in the skies.

Amiros, being one of the planets of Ektha, its parent star was well known for harboring an extremely vast array of bizarre life forms, creatures, and even monsters, ranging from crawling vegetation to gargantuan rocs and gigantic sea hydras. Because of all these, it was a place rich with exploration opportunities and mysteries, only waiting to be discovered by space explorers and capsuleers.

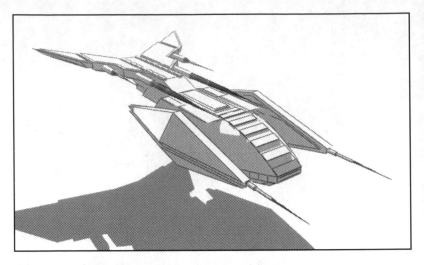

Rough sketch of a Hexiron class A frigate: *Heron*

For about two hours, their exploration went smoothly until suddenly, a violent shudder shook the entire frigate, shattering every glass, and throwing almost everything in it. The entire area immediately turned into a complete mess.

At the same time, loud emergency alarms also began sounding and ringing everywhere, together with repeated warning statements made by the artificial intelligence of the frigate, "Warning, engine failure at all chronium fuel cores. Warning, engine failure at all chronium fuel cores. Warning, engine . . ."

Twenty-six-year-old Keegan, who was piloting the frigate at its bridge, felt the violent tremors and immediately shouted while gripping tightly onto the side handles of his seat, "Whoa!"

He then quickly glanced through all the holographic screens along the control panels and realized that an explosion had occurred at the engine compartments, which was leaving behind a long trail of black fumes through the air.

In great distress, he exclaimed in agony, "What? How . . . how can this be? Shit!"

He then tried several ways to recover the engines by activating fire-extinguishing systems and restarting them. However, it was to no avail.

When Dusk who was at the back of the frigate, enjoying the view in his private accommodations felt the sudden shudder, he quickly dashed out into the main lobby at the center of the ship. There he saw twenty-three-year-old Raven using her PDA and ran to her, shouting, "Raven! What's happening?"

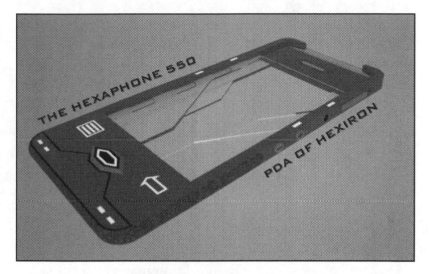

3D rendering of Raven's PDA

Raven quickly slid her PDA back into her pocket and answered, "Oh, Dusk! Relax, relax. I guess it's just an engine failure. I believe Keegan'll get it fixed soon."

Back on the bridge, Keegan still couldn't recover the engines, despite countless attempts.

"Crap! Why must this happen at this time? Ugh!" exclaimed Keegan in great fury. Having no other choice, he finally decided to crash-land the frigate. However, there was no suitable surface beneath, as he was still flying in the middle of an ocean, in which there were only small and bumpy islands.

Upon realizing this, Keegan groaned and made the final decision to settle on the nearest island instead.

"Crap, This is gonna be some really hard landing. I gotta let my friends know about this fast!"

Quickly, he turned the announcement system on and spoke.

"Dusk, Raven! This is Keegan! What you've just encountered is an engine failure. As I couldn't resolve it, I regret to say that we'll be crash-landing on the nearest island ahead of us!"

"What?" exclaimed Raven in absolute shock. "Isn't there another way to resolve this?"

"Keegan! You outta your mind?" exclaimed Dusk terrifyingly.

Keegan heard his friends and answered, "There's no other way! There probably won't be any more islands for me to land on if I continue to stay in the air! Besides, I don't wanna stall and let us all die! Hurry! Run for cover! This is gonna be a bumpy landing!"

Raven quickly looked into Dusk's eyes and exclaimed, "Hurry! Seek cover in your room while I seek cover in mine! Move!"

"All . . . alright!"

In a flash, Dusk and Raven disappeared into their respective private accommodations and braced for impact by hiding in a safe spot. Back on the bridge, Keegan slowed the frigate down and lowered its flaps and landing gear as it slowly descended, much like an airliner at the end of a flight.

"Come on, come on, come on . . ." murmured Keegan softly, hoping for a safe and successful landing.

At just 100 feet above the surface, the frigate flew past the beach of the island at a speed of 180 knots. A split second before touching down, Keegan quickly ducked down under the control panels and curled himself into a ball.

The frigate violently crashed against the sandy surface of the beach beneath and pummeled through the green vegetation deeper inside. The force of the crash was so monumental that the back half of the frigate literally broke off, exposing its interior.

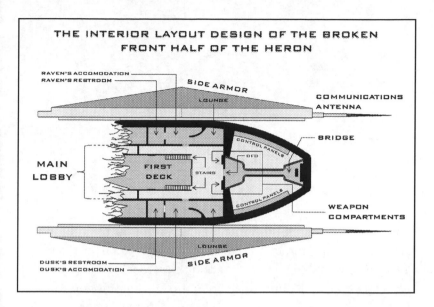

THE INTERIOR LAYOUT DESIGN OF THE BROKEN
FRONT HALF OF THE HERON

RAVEN'S ACCOMODATION
RAVEN'S RESTROOM

SIDE ARMOR

LOUNGE

COMMUNICATIONS
ANTENNA

CONTROL PANELS

BRIDGE

MAIN
LOBBY

FIRST
DECK

DFD

STAIRS

CONTROL PANELS

WEAPON
COMPARTMENTS

LOUNGE

DUSK'S RESTROOM
DUSK'S ACCOMODATION

SIDE ARMOR

CHAPTER 2

ESCAPE PLAN

The front half of the frigate continued sliding across the uneven ground, smashing through every rock and vegetation that came in its way before crashing into the thick buttress roots of a large tree. At the point of impact, it immediately came to a complete stop while its front hull sustained severe dents. Thereafter, there was total silence.

Dusk, who was hiding under his bed, slowly opened his eyes and couldn't believe what he saw. His room was completely thrashed to bits, with shattered glass everywhere. Distressed, he cried, "Oh, no . . . not this again!"

He then slowly crawled out, stood up, and cautiously made his way to the main lobby by taking small steps. To his utmost shock, the main lobby was also in the same state. Almost everything in it was completely deformed, destroyed, or shattered. Furthermore, half of the lobby was also exposed to the forested environment outside as the back half of the frigate had been ripped off.

Meanwhile, the danium fortified door (DFD) leading to the bridge slid opened. Dusk looked towards it and caught sight of Keegan slowly limping out in great pain.

"Ugghh!" groaned Keegan.

"Keegan!" exclaimed Dusk. "You okay?"

Keegan looked toward Dusk and answered in misery, "Argh . . . yeah! Don't worry, Dusk, I'm fine."

"You sure?"

Feeling dizzy, Keegan quickly held on to a railing ahead of him and answered, "Yeah! Just need . . . time to recover."

"Okay. Let me help you!"

As Dusk began jogging over to help him up, he caught sight of Raven appearing at the entrance of her accommodations and called, "Oh, Raven! You all right?"

"Yeah, perfectly fine. Took cover in a corner. How 'bout you?"

"Same. Keegan don't look so good. Let's help him up."

"Roger!"

The two ran over to Keegan and helped him stand firmly on his feet. Once he was feeling better, Keegan apologized to his friends. "Sorry about what just happened. The engine just . . . blew off, and there's nothing I could do to resolve it. Sorry, it's my fault. I should've inspected the ship more thoroughly before taking off."

Hurt by Keegan's words, Dusk answered, "Oh, don't say that, Keegan! People make mistakes and learn from them."

"But, I'm . . . really sorry."

Raven intervened. "Come on, Keegan, we're best friends, and we're all in this together."

Keegan pondered and answered, "You're right, Raven. Perhaps I should pick myself back up."

"There you go. Now, we need to find a way to get off this planet."

"But how?" said Dusk.

Keegan answered, "Let me make a call to the headquarters of the nearest Hexiron space station. Perhaps they could send a ship or something over to pick us up!"

"Okay, but . . . do you think they'll be able to find us in time?"

"What do you mean?"

"I mean, look around outside! This island is full of ravenous creatures, so I don't think it's wise to wait here for too long. We may need to move."

Raven said, "Dusk's right. They may just find our frigate, but not us."

"Hmm . . . so should I or should I not make the call?"

There was a moment of silence before Dusk finally agreed to Keegan's decision.

"Make the call; there's still a chance that they'll find us."

"Alright."

Keegan took his PDA from his pocket and accessed the "Contacts" application. Once inside, he scrolled through his list of contacts and made a call to the headquarters of the nearest Hexiron space station.

"Hello?"

"Hello! This is Keegan, a student from Telrux University in Acratum. Is this the headquarters of Skylon space station?"

"Yes, how may I help you?"

"My frigate malfunctioned and ended up crashing on a super-Earth called Amiros; parent star is Ektha. The name of the island is . . ."

Unsure what the name of the island was, Keegan quickly removed his PDA from his ear, looked at its holographic interface, and placed it back to his ear.

"Droughalis; requesting a dropship to pick me and two of my other friends up."

"Okay, where exactly on the island do you want the rescue dropship to be deployed?"

Unfamiliar with the island, Keegan just said the first thing that came into his mind, "Er . . . the tallest point on the island."

When Raven heard what Keegan just said, she mumbled loudly, "What? Do we know how to even get there?"

Quickly, Keegan signaled her to stop with his palm facing her and continued listening.

"Tallest point? Alright, But please . . . be careful out there. Amiros is home to all sorts of creatures that can kill humans. So if you get caught by them, I'm sorry to say that I can no longer help you. Is that understood?"

"Yes sir!" answered Keegan confidently.

"Great! Two dropships will be sent to your location in case something happens to one, so be ready. ETA 30 minutes."

"Two dropships? 30 minutes?"

Keegan received no response and ended the call by thanking, "Okay . . . thank you."

CHAPTER 3

LINE OF DEFENCE

Suddenly, the entire *Heron* frigate shook with a loud thud coming from outside. It appeared as though something heavy had collided against its external hull.

Alarmed by what just happened, the trio quickly looked around in silence.

"What was that?" exclaimed Dusk.

"I dunno . . . but I've got a bad feeling about this." said Raven.

The entire *Heron* shook once more with another loud thud, but this time coming from the part of the lobby that has been torn off.

Quickly, the trio looked towards where the sound came from and saw a gigantic green colored pear-shaped plant-like creature sitting just outside.

"Whoa! What's that?" exclaimed Dusk in surprise.

"It's . . . It's just a plant."

"But . . . but . . . it's moving!"

When Keegan and Raven observed the mysterious plant-like creature more closely, it appeared to be arranging its roots in such a way for a leap. Sensing that danger was imminent, Raven quickly stretched her left arm ahead of Dusk and Keegan, and shouted, "Stay back! It may be preying on us."

Suddenly, the plant-like creature abruptly jumped into the lobby and landed with another loud thud.

Aware that they were in grave danger, Raven quickly exclaimed, "Shit! It's coming for us! Quick! Grab your weapons!"

Dusk and Keegan loudly acknowledged at the same time, "Yes Raven!"

Quickly, the trio ran towards a weapons storage compartment located right next to the DFD leading to the bridge, and drew out weapons and ammunition.

When fully armed, they quickly returned to the railings and aimed their weapons at the gigantic pear-shaped plant-like creature, which was already starting to make another jump.

"We need to get outta here fast! Prepare to fire!" exclaimed Raven as they were strafing towards the stairs leading down.

"How did you know it's hostile?" exclaimed Keegan.

"You never know! Predatorial-like creatures without any form of sentience like this one are usually threatening! Better to be safe than sorry!"

"All right! Let me make the first shot then!"

Keegan, who was armed with a FT34 Phoenix freezethrower attached with a Plasma Vector Sight (PVS), a pair of forcefield generators, a position locker, and a Laser Aiming Device (LAD), activated the position locker and locked the weapon in free space. This was to absorb all of the weapon's recoil and weight. After which, with only one hand holding the heavy weapon, he squeezed the trigger and in the next moment, blue flames began gushing out from its muzzle.

Everything, including the railings nearby was immediately covered in ice. When the gigantic plant-like creature began experiencing severe frost bites, it quickly jumped towards where Keegan was standing.

"Keegan look out!" exclaimed Raven.

Quickly, Keegan dodged to one side while leaving his freezethrower still spatially locked in the air. At the same time, Dusk, who was armed with an M777 Wingman (assault rifle) attached with a JI72 digital scope, a pair of forcefield generators, and a Laser Aiming Device (LAD), pulled the trigger, discharging danium rounds (diamond bullets) at the plant-like creature.

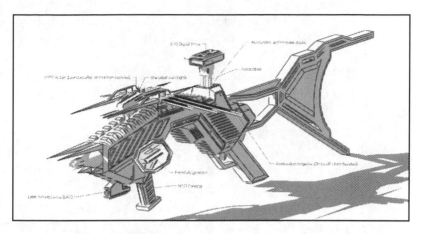

Rough sketch of the M777 Wingman assault rifle of Hexiron

Immediately, the plant-like creature, cracked into countless pieces of ice while still in mid-air.

The cracking sounds were no different from cracking glass, and were so loud that the trio quickly ducked for cover. After a moment of silence, they heard many more weird and awkward noises outside.

"EEEAAAOOOWWW! HOOH!"

"What did I just hear?" exclaimed Dusk fearfully.

"Crap! Looks like we've unnecessarily attracted the attention of more of them!" exclaimed Raven.

"What? Are you serious?" exclaimed Dusk.

Raven loaded a pair of rail magazines into her weapons as she spoke, "Oh come on Dusk! How can I not be serious in this kind of situation! Get ready! Expect a hoard of them sooner or later!"

"A hoard of them?"

"Then what do you think?"

Stunned, Dusk stared into Raven's eyes without saying a word.

"Keegan, you all right?" exclaimed Raven.

"Yeah! Much better now!" said Keegan while getting back on his feet.

"Excellent!"

Suddenly, about 10 more gigantic plant-like creatures emerged from outside. Quickly, Raven yelled to the top of her lungs, "SHOOT!"

"DUSK! I'LL FIRE FIRST! WHEN I RELOAD, YOU START FIRING! WE TAKE TURNS, OKAY?" exclaimed Raven.

"YES RAVEN!" exclaimed Dusk.

Without delay, Keegan quickly dashed back to his freezethrower, which was still spatially locked in the air and pulled its trigger, while Raven quickly aimed her two S84 Shatterer submachine guns, each attached with a Plasma Vector Sight (PVS), a suppressor, a flashlight, and a Laser Aiming Device (LAD) at the plant-like creatures and began discharging rail rounds.

3D renderings of danium shards (diamond bullets) of Hexiron

The overall suppressive fire was so potent that every single plant creature that passed through the boundary between the lobby and the environment outside was immediately frozen and cracked thereafter, resulting in a huge pile of ice accumulating at the scene.

When the number of plant creatures seemed to be increasing despite consistent suppression, Dusk threw a Blazer fragmentation grenade into the kill zone.

"Grenade!" shouted Dusk as he threw. When the grenade landed, the trio quickly ducked down for cover. The grenade exploded, killing numerous plant creatures at the same time while ricocheting ice fragments from the ground in all directions.

Dusk and his friends quickly stood back up and continued suppressing their fire. The kill zone was a total mess as more plant creatures were attracted and getting killed in frozen form by Keegan's deadly freezethrower.

Huge heaps and piles of frozen ice began accumulating till the exit became totally inaccessible. Nevertheless, the plant creatures never gave up in their pursuit for the trio.

"When will they stop? We'll run outta ammo if we continue like this!" exclaimed Dusk, but received no response.

Sooner later, Dusk's M777 Wingman depleted its last round on its last magazine.

"I'm outta ammo!" exclaimed Dusk.

He then aimed his assault rifle at the plant-like creatures ahead and pulled the trigger once more, this time launching the M777 Archer device attached above his weapon. It sped through the air at lightning speed, like an arrow shot from a bow, and instantly penetrated four targets in a single strike.

"EEEAAAOOOWWW!" wailed the plant creatures that were critically hit in excruciating pain.

Aware that their continuous firepower may not be sufficient to stop the plant-like creatures dashing in due to their overwhelming numbers, Dusk threw his assault rifle to the ground and began thinking of an alternate solution.

Shortly later, Keegan's freezethrower stopped spewing ice cold flames as his last canister ran out of fuel.

"Shit! I'm outta ammo!" exclaimed Keegan anxiously as he quickly deactivated the spatial locking mechanism on his weapon and dropped it to the ground. He then drew another weapon strapped on his back, the P89 Slicer minelayer (attached with a pair of forcefield generators) and fired two mines near the accumulated pile of ice.

As soon as the mines had landed, they detected nearby movement and immediately launched themselves back into the air vertically upwards. As soon as they were about to descend due to the pull of gravity, they exploded and unleashed horizontal rings of blades outwards in all directions parallel to the ground, literally slicing everything in their paths.

The mines were so potent that almost every single plant creature outside were literally sliced into two, some even three. As such, the entire area instantly became a total mess of gore and blood as organic juices spew everywhere. Even the interior walls of the *Heron* frigate sustained severe cuts that went as deep as three metres.

Suddenly, Dusk thought of an idea to escape and exclaimed, "Hey, I've got an idea!"

"What is it?" exclaimed Raven while still firing her sub machine guns.

"Gimme your PDA!"

"What? Why!"

"Just . . . give it to me!"

"Why should I?"

"Do you trust me?"

Raven gave no answer.

"Fine, have it your way!"

"Raven! Just pass it to him! Perhaps he has a great idea for us, like how it's always been!" exclaimed Keegan.

When Raven had depleted her last round on her last magazines, she pondered for some time, shrugged and hesitantly answered, "Alright, alright!"

She threw her sub machine guns to the lobby on the lower deck and took her PDA out. But then Dusk quickly snatched it away from her as soon as it left her pocket.

"Hey!" exclaimed Raven.

Realizing that no one was firing anymore weapons, Raven quickly drew another weapon strapped on her back, the M792 Hunter assault rifle. She loaded it with danium shards and continued remaining in high alert stance, although no more plant creatures were creeping in due to the heap of ice obstructing them.

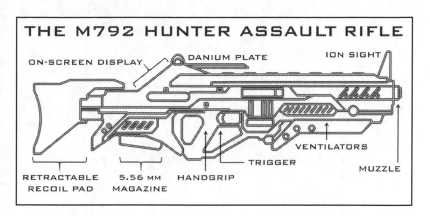

THE M792 HUNTER ASSAULT RIFLE

ON-SCREEN DISPLAY
DANIUM PLATE
ION SIGHT
RETRACTABLE RECOIL PAD
5.56 MM MAGAZINE
HANDGRIP
TRIGGER
VENTILATORS
MUZZLE

"Dusk! What're you doing!" exclaimed Raven.

"Hop on me!"

"Wha . . . what?"

CHAPTER 4

DRAGON'S WRATH

For some time, Raven received no response until suddenly, a loud and deafening roar of a fire-breathing wyvern thundered, "KHEEERRRHHH . . . !"

Shocked like never before, Keegan and Raven looked towards Dusk and were immediately stunned by what they saw. Dusk just literally transformed himself into a small wyvern (a fire breathing dragon).

"WWHHAATT? You mean you're gonna use Sparkie to smash through all the way out with us riding on your back?" exclaimed Raven in unparalleled astonishment.

"WHOA! What other ways can you think? I think Dusk did a great job! Hop on!" exclaimed Keegan.

Dusk, being in his dragon form lowered himself to allow his friends to climb onto his back. Keegan and Raven quickly strapped their weapons to their backs and ran towards Dusk.

When they reached him, they gradually made their way up by gripping onto the top surfaces of protruded scales and small spikes. After successfully climbing to the top, Keegan stretched his arm towards Raven and exclaimed, "Here, gimmie your hand!"

Raven extended her arm towards Keegan and was pulled up.

"There you go." said Keegan.

Dusk stood back up and ferociously roared, "KKHHEERRRHH . . . !"

"Hold on tight! This is gonna be one bumpy ride outta here!" exclaimed Keegan while gripping tightly onto Dusk's back fins.

Suddenly, Dusk dashed forward and smashed through the railings ahead, landing himself onto the lower deck beneath with a loud thud.

The landing was so hard that Keegan and Raven almost lost their grip. Nevertheless, they continued grabbing tightly onto Dusk's back fins with their eyes shut, hoping that everything would go according as intended.

Dusk roared once more and continued dashing forward.

"KHEEERRRHHH . . . !"

Without a hitch, he pummeled through the thick pile of ice, causing them to ricochet quickly into the air and scatter in all directions, resulting in an unprecedented mess.

"PPSSHHKKLLIIAANNGG! KANG . . . !"

Thereafter, dead plant bodies got stepped over, causing blood, goo, slime, and juices to squirt everywhere, while some of those that were still alive were violently smashed down or pushed away.

After dashing for some distance from the *Heron* frigate, all the pant-like creatures began diverting from the kill zone as they attempt to give chase. The number of plant creatures on the run was so monumental that the scene appeared as though a plant apocalypse had occurred.

While still grabbing hold of Dusk's back fin, Raven slowly opened her eyes, and was greatly astonished to see a sea of vegetation chasing towards her.

"HOLY SHIT!" exclaimed Raven.

Upon hearing Raven, Keegan also opened his eyes, saw what she saw and gave the same shocking reaction, "OHH MY GOD! OH . . . OH MY GOD!"

"DO SOMETHING!" exclaimed Raven.

As the plant creatures were also crawling very quickly, they eventually got closer to Dusk despite dashing at full speed. When Keegan saw this happening, he drew out his P89 Slicer minelayer from his back once more and began firing as many mines as he could to deter them to deter them as much as possible.

Without delay, all the mines that landed on the grassy ground jumped vertically back into the air and exploded with cutting edge plasma rings of blades, instantly slaughtering the numerous plant creatures that ran within its slicing radius.

"GHOAAZHAAZ! HAAZSH!" sounded the plant creatures in excruciating pain as they were sliced.

Realizing that what Keegan was doing was not sufficient to deter the hoard, Raven quickly drew her M792 Hunter assault rifle from her back with one hand, while still grabbing hold of one of Dusk's back fin with her other hand and fired danium rounds.

This time, the plant creatures giving chase behind became more aggressive as they began hopping instead of crawling fast.

Aware that their actions were to no avail, Keegan yelled in great desperation, "CRAP! They're getting closer, and gonna jump onto us!"

Dusk, who was still dashing as fast as he could heard Keegan's cry from his back and began breathing fire to the ground on both of his sides, leaving behind trails of burning inferno.

"HHHHHSSSSHHHHH . . . !" sounded Dusk's breath as scorching flames were ejected from his mouth.

Some of the plant creatures crawled through the fire and were immediately engulfed in flames.

"KWWAAI! KIAA!" sounded the plant creatures that got burned in intolerable pain, shot dead by Raven's assault rifle and slaughtered by Keegan's slicing mines.

Quickly, the plant creatures sensed the threat and began chasing Dusk from his sides while maintaining their continuous hops to avoid the heat, bullets, and slicing mines. By doing so, they could also land on Dusk's back and devour Keegan and Raven in an instant.

"DUSK! YOUR FLAMES AREN'T WORKING!" exclaimed Raven.

"CRAP!" exclaimed Keegan as he continued firing slicing mines.

Before Keegan knew it, he fired his last mine and exclaimed, "I'M OUTTA AMMO!"

Thereafter, he discarded his P89 Slicer minelayer weapon by throwing it into the chasing hoard. It flew and landed directly into a pear-shaped plant creature, killing it in an instant due to its great momentum.

"KHHYYAA!" sounded the plant creature in its excruciatingly painful death.

From this point on, Keegan became weaponless as he had discarded both of his primary (FT-34 freezethrower) and secondary (P89 Slicer minelayer) weapons. However, he still had one freezenade strapped on his belt.

Shortly later, Raven also depleted her last round in her last magazine.

"OUTTA AMMO! DUSK! DO SOMETHING ELSE! RUN FASTER! START JUMPING! FLY! OR WHATEVER TO LOSE THEM!" exclaimed Raven with great adrenaline and anxiety as the plant creatures were getting closer than she could ever imagine.

She then threw her assault rifle against the hoard and again, it landed right into another pear-shaped plant creature, killing it in an instant.

"EEEWYAA!" sounded the plant creature with a very alien-like voice.

Dusk, who was still dashing in his dragon form heard Raven's cry and realized that he hadn't been doing something which he could have done earlier.

"Wait a minute, I have wings! Ohh . . . !" thought Dusk within his mind.

Quickly, he opened his wings and began flapping them.

When Raven saw what Dusk was doing, she heaved a sigh of relief and exclaimed, "OH! About time!"

"OH! Finally . . ." heaved Keegan.

After flapping for some time, Dusk jumped into the air and began flapping even harder. Fortunately, he went airborne and began flying deeper into the island ahead. When he had reached an altitude where he was no longer reachable by the hoard of plant creatures beneath, Keegan and Raven continued heaving sighs of relief to themselves.

"OH . . . thank goodness Dusk! You . . . You did it . . . We did it . . . WE DID IT!" exclaimed Raven.

"HOAH . . . !" exclaimed Keegan while looking down and grabbing tightly onto Dusk's back fin.

Dusk managed to fly high and far enough till the hoard of plant creatures chasing from behind lost sight of him. However, he had no idea where to land, as he couldn't possibly leave the planet just by flying through its atmosphere. Nonetheless, he continued ascending and flying deeper into the island.

After spending some time in the air, Keegan said to Raven, "Raven! Does Dusk know where to fly to?"

"I believe so, cuz he was standing just right next to you while you were requesting for a rescue dropship from Skylon space station."

"Oh yes! Let's hope he does!"

Dusk overheard the conversation behind and remembered about where Keegan wanted the rescue dropship to be deployed to. As such, he began scouring through the entire island while talking to himself within his mind, "Oh yeah! The highest point of the island . . . the highest point . . . now where is it . . . come on . . . gotta find it . . ."

After surveying the entire island of Droughalis at 3,000 feet for some time, he saw three peaks. The highest one was a mountain at the other end of the island, which caught his attention.

"Bingo!" thought Dusk.

However, as he was about to align himself to the mountain, he heard a warning statement within his mind saying, "Warning, PDA battery level low. Changing of current morphology back to original half-human and half-Scentellian form imminent. Please return to your original form now to prevent unnecessary loss of data and errors."

Upon hearing this, Dusk became anxious as he was still flying high in the air. Keegan and Raven were completely unaware about this.

"What? Why must this happen at this time? Wait . . . Raven!" thought Dusk angrily.

Annoyed at Raven for using her PDA so frequently that it became low on battery power, he roared, "KHEERH!"

"Did you hear that?" said Keegan.

"It's just Dusk, he's probably tired. Don't worry."

"Okay."

In deciding in advance where to land, Dusk looked around and realized he was still flying high above a dense forest filled with odd-looking trees and vegetation.

"Oh man . . . how am I gonna land here. Come on, think . . . think!" thought Dusk fearfully as he had no idea whether if the trees beneath are dormant or dangerous.

Having no other choice, he concluded, "Oh well . . . I'd rather not die with my friends by falling from here. Gotta what I've gotta do."

Gradually, Dusk began descending slowly, so as to allow Keegan and Raven to maintain their stability and grip.

When Raven realized what Dusk was doing, she said to Keegan, "Hold on, why is Dusk descending? Shouldn't he be flying to that mountain over there?"

"Descending? Oh . . . looks like he had forgotten where we're supposed to be going."

Annoyed, Raven shouted at Dusk, "DUSK! DO YOU REMEMBER WHERE WE'RE GOING? WE'RE NOT SUPPOSED TO BE GOING DOWN NOW! CAN YOU HEAR ME?"

Dusk heard Raven yelling from behind and wanted to explain the reason, but was unable to because of his current form. Instead, he responded by roaring, "KHERH!"

"Dusk! You're flying lower and lower!" exclaimed Keegan.

"KHERH!"

Suddenly, Raven remembered that her PDA's battery was running low when Dusk took it. Furthermore, the "Morphology" application was also a quick energy drainer. Feeling regretful, she apologized loudly, "OH! Sorry! Sorry it's all my fault!"

"Why?" exclaimed Keegan.

"My PDA was running low on battery when Dusk took it, so he had to land now, otherwise . . . he would transform back to his original form here! In the air!"

"So that's why. Do you have any idea how dangerous it is to land here? Look down, do you think those trees are gonna give us a chance? Who told you to use your PDA so frequently? You never know when you need it during times like this!"

"I'm so sorry!"

When Dusk had descended through the thick canopy of odd-looking trees beneath, he kept looking straight to confirm whether if the ground ahead was safe for landing. But before he could do that, he had to first fly between two massive tree trunks.

CHAPTER 5

CREEPY CRAWLIE

Thinking that the path ahead was clear and therefore safe to proceed, Dusk continued gliding as per normal till suddenly, he got himself trapped in a gigantic cobweb connected between the two massive tree trunks, about 100 metres above the ground.

"KKHHEERRHH!" roared Dusk in absolute shock as he quickly began wriggling as hard as he could to free himself, but was to no avail. At the same time, he also thought about breathing fire to free himself, but decided not to, as it may once again unnecessarily attract the attention of the plant creatures inhabiting below.

"OH! WHAT'S . . . WHAT'S HAPPENING?" exclaimed Raven as she almost lost her balance.

"ARGH! COBWEB!" exclaimed Keegan.

Exhausted from all the wriggling, Dusk stopped moving and kept still.

Having a phobia of spiders, Raven became afraid and fearfully said, "Are . . . are there any spiders around? I hate spiders . . ."

"I dunno . . . just . . . keep your volume low."

"Okay . . ."

Thereafter, Raven caught sight of something black and huge moving in a dark cavern within the trunk of a large tree, but couldn't determine what it was. In fear, she exclaimed, "What . . . WHAT'S THAT?"

"What's what?"

When Keegan looked ahead and saw the same thing, he bellowed in utmost shock, "HOLY!"

Dusk also saw what his friends saw and began to fear. He then decided to breathe fire to deter it, but then he heard another warning statement within his mind saying, "PDA battery depleted, changing your current morphology back to original form now."

Before he could do anything else, thousands of highly refractive tessellations of hexagonal cells began appearing on all the surfaces of his dragon body, with buzzing sounds. Eventually, he became completely transparent like glass.

"BZZAZZAZZAZZAZZAZZAZZA . . . !"

When Raven saw what was happening, she quickly exclaimed in paralyzing fear, "What's, what's happening . . . no . . . NO! Please don't transform back Dusk! We still need you to burn THAT THING COMING!"

"CRAP!" exclaimed Keegan.

When Dusk had fully returned to his original form, Keegan and Raven fell from where they were and landed onto the cobweb beneath. Unfortunately, they got their hands stuck and were rendered immobile.

"EWW! This is sick! SICK!" exclaimed Raven in great disgust.

"Argh! Get it off me! Ugh!" exclaimed Keegan.

Dusk, who was already back in his original half-human and half-Scentellian form, slowly regained consciousness and opened his eyes. To his trepidation, he saw the entity drawing closer towards the entrance of the cavern.

"Dusk! Do something!" exclaimed Raven.

Dusk observed his hands and was surprised that they were still free from contact with the cobweb. Quickly, he took Raven's PDA out, but to his dismay, its battery was already flat.

"Man!" exclaimed Dusk.

Quickly, he kept Raven's PDA and took out his own. Once in the home screen, he scrolled through all the apps, desperately searching for the right one.

"Come on, come on, COME ON!" muttered Dusk.

This time, the large unknown creature crawled into the light, revealing its many eyes, long, black, and hairy legs, massive cephalothorax and abdomen. To everyone's unparalleled surprise, it turned out to be a gigantic tarantula, so huge that Raven lost control of her fear.

"AAARRRGGGHHH! SPIDER! DO SOMETHING!" exclaimed Raven in unprecedented terror.

Immediately after which, Dusk stumbled upon the "Consciousness manipulator" app and had an idea just in time. Quickly, he accessed the app by touching its icon on the holographic screen. Once inside, he saw the following options to choose from:

- Swapper
- Vegetator
- Hijacker

Unsure which option would be the best, Dusk analyzed each one carefully, "Swapper? Hmm . . . nope, don't wanna swap bodies with the spider. The spider'll still endanger my friends with my body. Vegetator? Hmm . . . the spider'll become motionless . . . sounds better but . . . how do we get down from here without anything to help us? Hijacker? Hmm . . . that's it!"

By the time Dusk had made up his mind, the tarantula already got so close to the trio that it began charging forward to devour them. Keegan and Raven, still stuck in the cobweb could do nothing, but yell in complete helplessness, "AAAARRRRGGGGHHHH!"

At the very moment when they were within the slicing zone of the spider's two frontal fangs, which were about to close in just a split second, Dusk managed to touch the "Hijacker" option while pointing the tip of his PDA at the tarantula just in time and immediately, his body became wobbly and motionless like a ragdoll, and fell into the cobweb face on.

The gigantic tarantula suddenly froze as its consciousness temporarily went into oblivion, and stopped moving, with Keegan and Raven still between its razor sharp fangs.

When Dusk slowly regained consciousness once again, he felt awkward, as he now had eight legs instead of the usual two, and an abdomen that has the ability to create threads of silk. Realizing that his friends were already partially between his fangs, and afraid of activating the wrong muscle, he tested by slowly widening them. To his surprise, it worked the same way as a human widening its mouth and crawled backwards.

At this point, Keegan and Raven were so overwhelmed with fear that they thought they were already dead. Therefore, they continued lying motionless on the cobweb with their eyes tightly shut.

Dusk kept a distance as he did not wish to scare them any further. When Keegan slowly began opening his eyes, the first thing he saw was Dusk's original body, which was lying motionless on the cobweb face down. Nonetheless, he never said a single word.

Thereafter, he looked ahead and caught sight of the gigantic tarantula sitting just right before him, with its anterior facing him. When he realized that he was still alive, he stared at it for some time in silence till he softly whispered to Raven, "Raven . . . are . . . are you there?"

Raven slowly opened her eyes and dizzily observed her surroundings. She saw large trees towering up into the skies above, with starlight filtering through the branches and leaves into numerous rays of light through the dusty air. To her complete astonishment, she realized she was still alive, "What . . . what . . . but . . . but I thought . . ."

When Raven looked ahead and saw the tarantula, she widened her eyes and was immediately rendered silent with terror once more.

After about five minutes, Keegan and Raven sensed that something must had happened, as the tarantula had been waiting at the same spot all the time without moving.

Keegan cautiously and softly whispered to Raven, "Wait a minute . . . I thought . . . I thought the spider just came to finish us off?"

When Raven's fear had slightly subsided, she continued her silence for a while more and softly whispered back, "I . . . dunno . . . Maybe . . . maybe we're already dead."

"How do you know?"

"Do you know you're dreaming, when you're dreaming?"

"No . . . but, but I really don't think we're dead. Wait a minute . . . could it be Dusk? How could he possibly just die here, when the spider haven't even reached him."

"Hmm . . ."

"Why don't you call out to the spider, see if it responds positively."

"The hell would I do that."

"Why not?"

"You really wanna risk doing that?"

"I know how you feel. But, we'll never know till unless we try."

"I'm not gonna do it."

"Okay . . . then, I'll do it."

"No . . . don't!"

Keegan called out to the spider, "DUSK! IS THAT YOU? IF IT'S YOU, NOD YOUR HEAD AND TURN YOURSELF AROUND!"

Dusk, still in control of the spider nodded his head and turned himself around.

Upon seeing the positive response, Keegan exclaimed in great relief, "IT'S DUSK! OH THANK GOODNESS!"

Stunned, Raven bellowed, "OH REALLY?"

"Yeah! It just did what I said!"

"Oh thank God! BUT, I STILL HATE SPIDERS!

When Dusk began turned back and began crawling forward to his friends, Raven got so terrified that she lost control of her fear once more and screamed, "AARRGGHH! GET AWAY!"

"Raven chill! Chill! It's Dusk! Don't worry!"

"I HATE SPIDERS! GET IT AWAY FROM ME!"

Seeing that Raven's has been frightened, Dusk stopped crawling and stood still.

"Raven! For crying out loud! PLEASE! If you're gonna continue behaving like this, I think we'll all be dead when Dusk's time of controlling the spider expires! THINK!"

Raven stopped screaming and kept silent. After thinking through what Keegan had said, she apologized, "Sorry . . . I . . . I'm just very afraid of spiders."

"Then just close your eyes and bear with it!"

"Okay, okay!"

When Raven closed her eyes, Dusk continued crawling forward. When he got close enough, he stretched his two frontal limbs forward and placed their tips at Keegan's sides in the attempt to pull him out.

"Ouh!" exclaimed Keegan the moment Dusk's limbs had gripped him by his waist.

Gradually, Dusk lifted Keegan up and pulled him out from the cobweb, leaving behind long trails of silk still stuck onto him.

"Don't worry Raven! Everything's gonna be okay!" exclaimed Keegan while being lifted.

Dusk placed Keegan on his back and began doing the same to Raven. But when his two frontal limbs got into contact with Raven, she screamed uncontrollably, "AARRGGHH!"

Scared by her abrupt scream, Dusk quickly released his limbs from her. Keegan saw what happened and exclaimed, "RAVEN! REMEMBER WHAT I TOLD YOU!"

Raven remembered that it was Dusk who was pulling her and became silent thereafter. When ready, Dusk slowly moved his limbs back towards Raven. Enduring her fear to the best she can this time, Raven did not make any noise when Dusk's limbs got into contact with her waist. Gradually, she was pulled up, and out from the cobweb, also leaving behind long trails of silk still stuck onto her. When Dusk landed Raven on his hairy back, she reopened her eyes and saw Keegan sitting right next to her.

"Well done Raven." said Keegan.

Still in fear, Raven responded by just nodded her head without saying a word, as she was sitting on one of her most feared creatures.

"Just hold on tight, and we'll see it goes."

Dusk surveyed the area one last time and saw his own body lying motionless and face down against the cobweb right next to his PDA. With his limbs, he gripped its waist and raised it up. When Raven saw Dusk's dark and hairy limbs moving over her, she panicked and widened her eyes, but did not scream or shout. Instead, she called out to Keegan, "Keegan!"

"Yes Raven!"

"What's he doing now?"

"Er . . . that must be Dusk's body. Quick, grab it!"

"Eww! That's sick!" exclaimed Raven in disgust, as Dusk's body was covered in silk, like a mummy.

"Come on Raven, I'll do it with you."

Keegan and Raven stretched their hands out and held onto Dusk's original body to place it near them while Dusk was lowering it. Once done, Keegan praised Raven for her effort, "Well done Raven."

Raven gave no response.

Thereafter, Dusk brought his limbs back to the front and gripped his PDA out from the cobweb. When Raven saw the limbs moving over her for the second time, she panicked again once more and kept her eyes locked at it till its tip stopped right ahead of her face.

Keegan saw what was happening and said to Raven, "He seems to be passing to you something, look closely!"

Raven strained her eyes while looking between the two limbs and saw a small device sandwiched between them.

"What's that?" said Raven.

"That's Dusk's PDA! Careful! It has the power to make this spider come back to life and kill us, so don't meddle with it!" exclaimed Keegan.

"Okay! But eww!"

Slowly, she stretched her arms upwards and grabbed hold of Dusk's PDA, which was covered in silk and kept it in her pocket. Dusk then brought his limbs back to the front and thought about descending to ground level, but didn't know how to. So, he ended up staring down for some time, thinking of a way to do it by talking to himself within his mind, "Can I crawl down the trunk of this tree? Or should I just . . . jump down?"

When he finally realized that he has the ability to create strains of silk, he released a trail of cobweb from the back of his abdomen and gradually began crawling to the edge of the web.

As his body was becoming vertical to the ground, Keegan exclaimed, "Quick! Grab onto something!"

Keegan and Raven quickly grabbed a bunch of hair on Dusk's back. When the anterior of Dusk's spider body began facing vertically downwards, he visually scanned the ground beneath to ensure that it was clear and free from threats. After confirming safe, he continued excreting strains of silk from his abdomen to the cobweb beneath his hind legs to firmly attach to it. Thereafter, he began lowering himself by dangling from the strains of silk while slowly extending it.

As he nears the ground beneath, he sensed danger and stopped descending. At this point, he was only about 12 metres above the ground.

"What's happening?" Raven mumbled.

Keegan did not answer.

After dangling for some time, Dusk and his friends caught sight of an awkward-looking snake-like creature emerging from the vegetation beneath. It has two heads, one on each end of its body and moves by slithering forward in an s-shaped manner.

"Oh my god . . . what is that!" exclaimed Raven while looking down.

"It . . . it looks like a giant snake!"

"Giant snake!? Then . . . how're we gonna get down?"

"Err . . . I have a bad feeling about this."

To the trio's surprise, the snake-like creature turned out to be a double headed cobra without a rattle. Not knowing what to do, Keegan and Raven waited for Dusk to make his next move.

Aware that the size of the spider was much larger than the alien cobra, Dusk cut off the strains of silk behind his abdomen by slicing it with the sharp organic blades on his hind limbs and before he knew it, he began free falling downwards.

When Raven felt the sudden falling sensation, similar to the feeling of riding a dropping roller coaster, she made a short, loud and sharp scream, "Aargh!"

"Whoa!" bellowed Keegan.

During the fall, Dusk pointed the tips of all his eight limbs at the alien cobra beneath. Eventually, he landed directly and hardly onto the center of the body of the alien cobra, crushing it with unprecedented fatality. Blood, goo, and organic juices squirted and spewed everywhere, rendering the whole area a total mess of gore.

"KKHHEE!" sounded the cobra in its excruciatingly painful and instant death. Shocked by what Dusk just did, Keegan and Raven bellowed, "WWHHOOAA!"

Thereafter, Dusk stood motionless for a moment, with all his limbs still pierced through the body of the alien cobra, making it appear just like an insect, pierced on a stick for display.

Convinced that the creature had been killed, he slowly removed his limbs, one by one onto the ground. While doing so, long strands of slime and blood became visible, sticking between his limbs and the creature.

When Dusk has had all his limbs out, he slowly crawled to a safe distance and lowered his body to allow his friends to dismount safely.

"Should . . . should we get down?" mumbled Raven.

To determine if it was safe to dismount, Keegan assessed the environment for potential threats before answering, "Well . . . I think it's safe. For now, the only threat I see is this monster we're sitting on!"

"But it's Dusk!"

"Yes, but imagine what could possibly happen if his consciousness suddenly jumps back to his body because of a time limit or something! You never know!"

"Oh! Okay, okay. Let's get down then!"

As Raven began making her way down slowly, Keegan assisted her by grabbing her hand while also climbing down at the same time.

"Slow and steady Raven, you can do it." said Keegan.

"Thanks Keegan! You can let go now."

When the two friends of Dusk finally had their feet back on the ground, Keegan realized Dusk's dormant body was still lying motionless on the back of the tarantula.

"Shit we forgot about Dusk!" exclaimed Keegan.

Confused, Raven answered, "Dusk? What do you mean?"

Keegan pointed his finger to the top of Dusk's spider body and Raven exclaimed, "Oh crap! How do we get it down?"

When Dusk heard the conversation between his friends, he raised his two frontal limbs to his back, gripped his body and gradually carried it down. When Keegan saw this, he said to Raven, "Forget it Raven, Dusk's doing it now."

"Oh . . . okay."

Once Dusk had gently placed his original body onto the ground, he thought within his mind, "Okay . . . jobs done . . . time for me to switch back."

Suddenly, another thought struck his mind, "Wait! If I return to my own body now, wouldn't the spider kill me and my friends? Hmm . . . I guess I'll do it elsewhere . . ."

When Dusk began crawling away from his friends, Keegan became aware about his intention of reverting his consciousness back to his own body, as the spider was no longer needed. When Raven began following Dusk, he quickly stretched his arm ahead of her and stopped her after her first step was made.

"Hey!" exclaimed Raven.

"Do you have any idea what Dusk's about to do now?"

Uncertain, Raven answered with the first thing that came into her mind, "Urm . . . pee?"

Disappointed with her response, Keegan smacked his forehead with his palm and said, "Oh good grief! He's intending to switch back to his own body, but he can't do it here, as the spider'll kill us! So he had to do it elsewhere, get it?"

"Oh! Yes Keegan . . ."

"Your fear of spiders has seemed to cause you to lose confidence like you had earlier. You must overcome it. Okay?"

"Oh . . . okay."

Keegan and Raven remained at where they were, anxiously waiting for Dusk's original body to open his eyes.

When Dusk had crawled behind a large boulder where his two friends were no longer visible, he rolled his eyeballs clockwise 10 times and closed them for about 10 seconds, as it was a way to revert his consciousness back to his own body.

After doing this for some time, he felt as though his soul was leaving the tarantula's massive body, and floating back to his own—a total out of body experience.

When he began regaining consciousness, he gradually opened his eyes and felt very dizzy. When Keegan saw Dusk reawakening, he exclaimed in great relief, "Dusk! You're back!"

Dusk gave Keegan a tired look, smiled and mumbled, "Yes Keegan."

CHAPTER 6

TIME BALL

When Keegan looked afar, he caught sight of the gigantic tarantula which Dusk was in control previously, crawling out from the massive boulder. As fear began to arise once more, Keegan very carefully called out to his friends while maintaining his volume, "Er . . . guys . . ."

Dusk and Raven heard Keegan's call, looked into his eyes, and looked into the direction he was facing. Dusk, who was sitting on the ground with his legs straightened, widened his eyes in shock, looked at Raven, placed his index finger onto his lips and hissed at her as a sign to be silent and stay low, "Shhh."

Raven nodded her head while they slowly knelt down to keep a low profile.

Unfortunately, the gigantic tarantula sensed the dead alien cobra behind and stopped crawling. In the next moment, it turned itself around and caught sight of the trio with its small black eyes.

Grappled with fear and anxiety, Keegan said in paralyzing terror, "Guys? Are . . . are you seeing what I'm seeing?"

Overflowed with fear, Raven looked into the spider and abruptly screamed, so loud that it unnecessarily caught the attention of all the plant creatures inhabiting around, "AAARRRGGGHHH! DO SOMETHING DUSK!"

Too weak to do anything, Dusk exclaimed, "I . . . I'm not feeling so good. Keegan! Find a way to get us outta this fast! Come on I trust you!"

"What? Why me?"

"Come on Keegan, look at Raven. She's already too paranoid to do any good."

Keegan reluctantly answered, "Okay, okay!"

He then looked everywhere and saw everything (plants, vines, leaves, etc . . .) around moving and wriggling. In addition to the awareness that his friends were now solely depending on him to survive, he felt stressed and mumbled to himself, "Oh man, oh man . . ."

Quickly, he slid his PDA out from his pocket and scrolled through all the apps in it. Somehow, he stumbled upon the "Stasis" app and heaved a quick sigh of relief, "Ah! Yes!" and opened it with a touch of his finger.

The application opened in a flash, displaying two options to choose from:

- Speed up
- Slow down

When he saw that some of the plant creatures were already charging towards him, he quickly selected the "Speed up" option and pointed the tip of his mobile device to the ground between himself and his other friends.

When he activated the app with a touch of his finger, a massive, transparent, and highly refractive hemisphere of plasma membrane filled with hexagonal tessellations immediately appeared from the point on the ground where he had pointed and expanded till it completely covered the trio, forming something like a bubble shield.

Inside this hemisphere, time passes a thousand times faster than the time outside. Therefore, if you were inside it, the time outside would pass a thousand times slower, implying that everything you see outside would appear to be frozen.

After the stasis shield has been fully spawned, there was a moment of silence among the trio. Keegan observed everything outside and saw that they were all frozen. The tarantula, plant creatures, twigs, vines and everything else were completely motionless, as though they had been spatially locked for display in a museum.

Feeling contented for what he had done, Keegan smiled and joyfully exclaimed, "Yeah!"

Keegan's two other friends saw what he did and also heaved a sigh of relief.

"Whoa . . ."

CHAPTER 7

MOBILE TOILET

Meanwhile, Dusk called out to his friends in a rather fearful tone, for the time was now finally right for what he has been wanting to do, "Err . . . guys . . . ?"

"Yes Dusk?" Raven answered.

"I . . . I need to pee . . . but I don't have the app to do it."

Stunned, Keegan exclaimed, "What?"

"I need to pee now, it's urgent!"

Raven quickly looked at Keegan and exclaimed, "See Keegan! I told you Dusk wanted to pee."

Annoyed, Keegan answered, "Urgh . . . all right!"

"Sorry." Dusk apologized.

Reluctantly, Keegan accessed the "Portal" application in his PDA, followed by the "Urinal" option. Eventually, a portal leading to a toilet bowl opened on the interface of his mobile device. When he handed the device over to Dusk, he quickly grabbed it and said, "Thanks Keegan! Now will you two mind looking away? Thanks!"

When Keegan and Raven turned themselves around, Dusk unzipped his pants and urinated through Keegan's PDA. While doing so, he maintained his stream at the center of the portal to avoid wetting the sides.

Worried that his PDA might be stained, Keegan said to Dusk while still facing away, "Remember to aim properly! I don't wanna have a stinky phone!"

"Okay!"

When Dusk was done, he shouted, "Done!"

Keegan turned back, retrieved his PDA and observed it. To his surprise, his mobile device was completely free from any stains.

"Wow . . . not bad Dusk, you should've signed up for the sniping course in the Hexagon!"

Dusk laughed, "Haha Keegan! Stop exaggerating!"

Keegan smiled and kept his PDA.

CHAPTER 8

IDEAS AND PLANS

The silence between the trio went on as they continued staring at each other, not knowing what to do next. Meanwhile, Keegan took the first step to say something, "Why . . . why're you guys staring at me like this?"

No one answered.

"Come on guys, you're starting to freak me out."

Suddenly, Dusk said, "We gotta do something quick, else this shield's gonna disappear!"

"What're we gonna do?" exclaimed Keegan.

Dusk pondered for some time before coming to a conclusion, "How about we continue searching through our PDAs? I believe there's a way! Alright, I'll browse through mine, while you browse through yours. Deal?"

Satisfied with Dusk's idea, Keegan agreed, "Sounds like a plan!"

Suddenly, Raven shouted at Dusk, "Hey! Don't you dare to that!"

Confused, Dusk answered, "What? Do what?"

"That's my PDA you're a out to use! Use yours!"

"Oh! Thanks for the reminder, I almost forgot . . . here."

"Alright . . ."

Dusk and Raven exchanged for their own PDAs. Once done, Dusk said to Raven, "Don't turn it on yet, okay? It's still low on power."

"Okay."

When Dusk and Keegan were ready with their PDAs, they browsed through all the apps in their mobile devices for a solution. After browsing through everything thrice, Keegan was still uncertain which would be the best. As his heart began pounding faster, he said to Dusk in a rather worried tone, "Dusk . . . I don't think I've found any good one. How boutchyou?"

Dusk, still scrolling through his PDA answered, "Hold on . . . er . . . nope. But by looking at our current situation, the only way we can escape from here is up."

"Up?"

"Yeah!"

"But how?"

"That's why I need you to help me with this fast before this shield ruptures!"

Keegan continued thinking about Dusk's suggestion and finally thought of an idea, "Hey, how about, er . . . how about we use, use . . . use a Dr . . . dr . . . Deamstick!"

"Dreamstick? OH YEAH! But . . ."

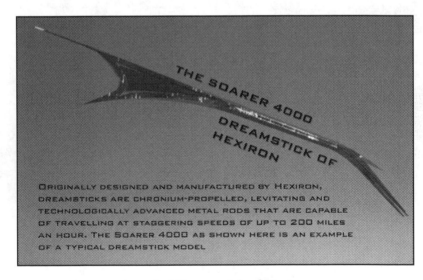

ORIGINALLY DESIGNED AND MANUFACTURED BY HEXIRON, DREAMSTICKS ARE CHRONIUM-PROPELLED, LEVITATING AND TECHNOLOGICALLY ADVANCED METAL RODS THAT ARE CAPABLE OF TRAVELLING AT STAGGERING SPEEDS OF UP TO 200 MILES AN HOUR. THE SOARER 4000 AS SHOWN HERE IS AN EXAMPLE OF A TYPICAL DREAMSTICK MODEL

A typical Dreamstick of Hexiron

"But what?"

"But we'll have to wait till this shield ruptures first!"

"Why! Can't we just fly out of it?"

"Of course not! Haven't you taken a course on stasis physics in the Hexagon before?"

"Nope."

Dusk sighed and gave Keegan a short lecture, "Okay . . . listen. The difference in time passing rates between outside and in here would literally tear our Dreamstick apart if it passes through the membrane of this stasis shield. This meant that we have to be extremely careful if we were to be waiting on our Dreamstick for it to rupture. A slight movement from you, me or Raven would cause it to accelerate abruptly. And also, if we're too slow to react to the rupturing of this shield, the creatures outside will most likely reach us! I mean . . . look outside! Look at how close they are and how fast they could possibly be moving!"

"Alright . . . so . . . are we still gonna go with that idea?"

"I dunno . . . what do you think?"

"Hmm . . ."

After pondering for some time, Keegan thought of idea and exclaimed, "I've got another idea!"

Dusk and Raven quickly glanced at Keegan and bellowed, "What is it?" at the same time.

"Okay . . . how about I turn all of us invisible. I have the app to do it. When the shield ruptures, the creatures outside would think that we've already escaped, and will therefore stop coming for us. What do you think?"

Dusk and Raven continued staring blankly at Keegan.

"Keegan, do you think the plants outside are that stupid? I don't think it's gonna be that simple." said Raven.

"Raven's right. I think you need to think more than that Keegan. Raven, do you have any suggestions?" said Dusk.

Raven answered, "Well, I remember seeing the "Inferno" app in your phone. Its icon is sort of like an orange flame or something. Perhaps you could use it to set them on fire. Might buy us some time to escape later."

"Hmm . . . but it also depends on how we're escaping. Anyway, good point! Shall give that a shot now."

Dusk searched through his home page and found the "Inferno" app. He then accessed it with a touch of his finger and pointed the tip of his mobile device at the hoard of plant creatures outside. When his thumb was already just above the activation button, he said, "Ready?"

"Go!" exclaimed Raven.

Dusk activated the app, and saw a spark of fire appearing on where he had pointed. It appeared to be frozen due to the substantially slower time passing rate outside. It was only just created at the very instant of time.

Furthermore, his battery power was also instantly drained by about 5%, as the fire comes from the energy stored within his PDA.

"Take this, and this, and . . . this!" exclaimed Dusk as he created multiple sparks of fire on the plant creatures around him. He had so much time that he even created some sparks at the center of the eyes of some of the plant-like creatures.

When he saw the gigantic tarantula at the back, he created another spark on it and exclaimed, "And especially you!"

After draining a total of about 40% of the energy of his PDA, Dusk exited the application and said, "Alright, that should be enough. Now . . . any other ideas?"

"Other than burning them, perhaps you could also slow them down." said Raven.

"How?"

"The "Momentum reducer" app, do you have it?"

"Hmm . . . let me see."

Dusk scrolled through his home screen once more and saw the app which Raven was talking about.

"Found it!" exclaimed Dusk.

He then accessed it with a touch of his finger and again, he pointed the tip of his mobile device at the plant creatures outside.

When he activated the app, nothing seemed to have happened, because forces cannot be seen with just the naked eye. But he was still confident that it had worked, as the battery level of his PDA continued draining by about 2% after each activation.

When he had done this to almost all the plant creatures outside, he exited the app and said, "Okay, that's enough. Any other ideas?"

Keegan thought of one, and exclaimed, "Oh . . . oh! I have another!"

"What is it?" said Dusk.

"How about I teleport all of us to somewhere far from here?"

Dusk shook his head sideways and answered, "Er . . . maybe not."

"Why?"

"Look around you! Can you see where you wanna go? This place is already such a mess!" said Raven.

Thereafter, Dusk accessed the "Local radar" app and saw that he and his friends had been surrounded by countless red dots, which represent each threat up to a hundred metres away. Shocked, he exclaimed, "Oh my god! We've been surrounded by 100 metres of plant creatures! Think of something quick Keegan! Don't leave all the work to Raven!"

Dusk exited the app and continued searching for another app.

Meanwhile, Keegan thought of another idea and exclaimed, "I've got another idea!"

"Shoot!" exclaimed Dusk.

"Okay here goes . . . we'll still proceed with your idea of going up as usual, okay? Except that it'll be a little different this time."

"Okay . . . we're listening." answered Dusk.

"Good . . . first, I'll shrink the three of us to as small as an ant."

Shocked with what Keegan just said, the two widened their eyes and exclaimed, "WHAT?"

After a moment of silence, Dusk said to Keegan in a worried tone, "Are you serious? What for?"

"Er . . . I'm not done yet."

"Oh! Sorry er . . . carry on."

"So! As I was saying . . . first, I'll shrink all of us. Then, I'll transfer the data of one of my Dreamsticks in my PDA out into its physical form. See the link to our previous idea?"

Dusk and Raven nodded their heads as though they were listening to a boring lecture.

"Alright, then we'll board the Dreamstick together and fly close to the surface of this shield at high speeds, such that when it disappears, we can just simply fly out straightaway without having to risk accelerating from stationary position. Furthermore, since we're also small, we're also less likely to be caught by the creatures outside."

After listening to Keegan's so called "lecture", Raven looked at Dusk and said to him, "So . . . what do you think?"

Dusk looked into Raven's eyes, pondered for some time and thought, "Well, I dunno but, this shield's gonna rupture anytime soon so . . . I guess we'll just let him go with his idea. See if it works out."

Raven shrugged, then called out to Keegan, "Okay . . . Keegan!"

"Yeah?"

"Just do whatever you've planned to do. We don't have much time left."

"Yes Raven!"

As Keegan was thirsty, he quickly accessed the "Waterer" app and activated it while pointing his PDA upwards at an angle towards him. When a stream of water began launching from the tip of his mobile device, as data was constantly transferred into physical water, he landed the other end of the stream into his mouth, like drinking from a water cooler.

Once his thirst has been quenched, he exited the app, and accessed the "Shrinker" app, which displayed the following options to choose from:

- Whole
- Head only

He selected "Whole" and pointed the tip of his PDA towards Dusk first.

"Dusk, I'll shrink you first, ready?" said Keegan.

"Wait."

Dusk quickly kept his PDA and When ready, he said, "Okay, go!" and braced for what was about to happen by shutting his eyes.

"Alright, here goes nothin'!"

Keegan activated the app with a touch of his finger, and before he knew it, strange sounds began emanating from Dusk as he gradually began shrinking in size. While this was happening, Keegan and Raven couldn't get their eyes off him.

When Dusk had shrunk to about the size of a grape fruit, he looked up to his two friends and was astounded by how small he was. His friends were gargantuan in size!

"Whooaa . . ." awed Dusk.

Thereafter, Keegan looked at Raven and said to her, "You ready?"

Anticipating for the shrinking experience, Raven gave a slight smile and nodded her head with her eyes shut. Without further delay, Keegan did the same to her, and she began emanating the same strange noises as Dusk did while he was shrinking.

When she had shrunk to the same relative size as Dusk, Keegan took a deep breath, braced himself for the supernatural, shut his eyes, and rotated his PDA till its tip was pointing towards his chest. When ready, he took a deep breather and bravely activated the application.

When the trio had finally been shrinked, Keegan observed his environment and was bewildered by how small he and his friends were. From this, he mumbled to himself in overwhelming awe, "Whooaa . . . this is really, really small."

"Wow . . . I've never seen anything like it." said Dusk.

CHAPTER 9

ANT WAR

After spending some time admiring the sheer size of everything around, Keegan closed the "Shrinker" app, and then accessed the "Storage" app in the attempt to transfer the data of one of his Dreamsticks out into physical form.

But then suddenly, two blade-like fangs protruded from the sandy soil beneath, clamped Keegan's right leg and forcefully pulled him down into the soil.

"Ar . . . arh!" exclaimed Keegan as he lost his balance, fell and dropped his PDA.

"ARH! SOMETHING GOT ME! HELP!" wailed Keegan in sudden terror as his right leg sank deeper into the soil.

Dusk and Raven saw what was happening and exclaimed in great shock, "OH! Keegan!"

Quickly, they ran over and caught hold of his arms. They then attempted to pull him back up with all their might.

"PULL! PULL! HARDER!" exclaimed Dusk.

"I'M TRYING, I'M TRYING!" exclaimed Raven.

However, the pull by the unknown entity in the ground was so strong that their efforts in rescuing Keegan were to no avail. As such, they also ended up being pulled into the soil.

"MAN! WE'RE GONNA SINK IN IF WE DON'T PULL HARDER!" exclaimed Dusk as he began sinking downwards too.

"THIS IS ALREADY THE BEST I CAN DO DUSK! ARGH!" exclaimed Raven.

"COME ON, WE CAN'T LET HIM DIE HERE!"

Fortunately, Keegan stopped sinking, but as the amount of force that Dusk and Raven were exerting on the ground was so great, it just literally gave way and collapsed, unveiling a large colony of gigantic purple ants beneath.

"AARRGGHH!" exclaimed the trio as they were falling with the sand.

When they had landed onto the collapsed sand beneath, they looked around in dizziness. To their shocking dismay, they realized they had been surrounded by purple ants. Their sizes range from as small as a mustard seed to as large as half of a human fist.

"What? Ants? Why . . . why're they so big? AARRGGHH! Stay away from me!" screamed Raven in terror.

Dusk quickly stood back up, and said, "Quick, get up!"

Raven quickly did what Dusk had commanded, but Keegan fell back on the ground due to the wound on his right leg.

"ERARGH!" wailed Keegan in excruciating pain

Dusk saw the state which Keegan was in and said to him, "It's okay Keegan, just hang in there. We'll cover you!"

Thereafter, he swung his Danium Sword strapped on his back forward, into his right hand and activated its energy blades, which were corrosive edges along the blades of the sword.

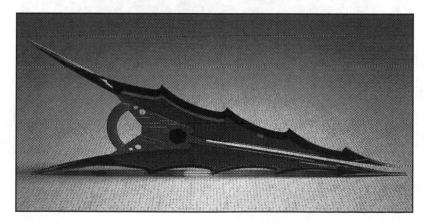

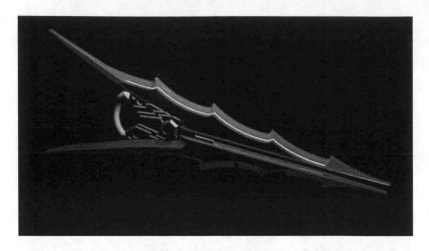

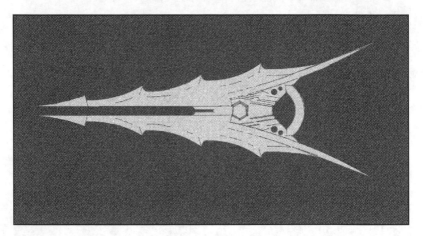

**The dazzling Danium Sword of Hexiron with
its energy blades activated. Rendering (top and
bottom left) and sketch (bottom right)**

"TTSSHH!" sounded Dusk's Danium Sword as its corrosive
and sharp edges were lit up brightly.

As a further defensive measure, two additional cutting edge
danium blades also appeared at the two sides of the sword, spatially
locked in free space relative to its blades.

Once armed and ready, Dusk quickly faced the ants opposite
Raven and got into high alert position.

Keegan continued wailing in excruciating pain on the ground between his two friends due to the deep cuts in his legs.

"HOLD THIS POSITION!" exclaimed Dusk.

Fearing that his Danium Sword may not be sufficient to deter the ants, Dusk quickly drew another weapon strapped on his back, the RP3 Rocket Pistol attached with a Plasma Vector Sight (PVS), a pair of forcefield generators, and a Laser Aiming Device (LAD), which he obtained from the Heron frigate earlier.

"Keegan! Here! Grab this!"

Dusk threw the rocket pistol to Keegan, and he caught it.

"Got it!" exclaimed Keegan.

"Raven! Need a weapon?" exclaimed Dusk.

"Yes!"

Quickly, Dusk took his PDA out with his other hand and accessed the "Storage" application. There, he selected the Scentellian plasma-based directed energy weapon, also known as the plasma repeater "H17 Hadal Rifle" and pointed its tip on where Raven was standing.

A green colored holographic projection of the weapon appeared between Raven's feet, indicating that it can be placed.

Without further ado, Dusk tapped "Place object", and the hologram disappeared. Immediately, transparent and highly refractive hexagonal tessellations began appearing at the same spot, bearing the shape of the weapon while emanating buzzing sounds, as data were converted into physical mass.

When the Hadal Rifle had been fully formed, Raven quickly weld it in her arms, while Dusk quickly returned to high alert stance.

Suddenly, one of the larger ants took a few steps forward and began crawling faster, causing the rest to follow.

Quickly, Raven aimed her plasma repeater at the ants and began spraying superheated plasma bolts.

Dusk raised his sword and braced himself for a slicing rampage.

Although Keegan was already armed with a rocket pistol, he did not fire it, as he feared that the explosion might kill he and his friends due to its large blast radius and how close the ants could possibly be.

After firing for some time, the rate of fire of Raven's plasma repeater gradually decreased as it was heating up. Nevertheless, the ants on her side were effectively suppressed, as the superheated plasma bolts burnt through their hulls and limbs. Some were even instantly killed from direct headshots.

As Dusk wasn't armed with a weapon that shoots, the ants on his side managed to reach him first. When the first soldier ant got within his reach, he forcefully swung his Danium Sword from his right to his left, slicing through its two gigantic mandibles.

"AARRGGHH!" yelled Dusk as he forcefully swung his sword.

Immediately, the soldier ant squealed in excruciating pain, "EEEKKK . . . !" as goo and organic juices spewed out from the sliced cross sectional area. Quickly, Dusk swung his sword once more and sliced through its left frontal limb. Unbalanced, the soldier ant fell to the ground and become immobile.

"EEEKKK AAAKKK . . . !" the soldier ant continued squealing.

Thereafter, the rest of the ants behind quickened their pace and clustered into a swarm. When Dusk saw this, he became overwhelmed with so much anxiety and stress that he began swinging his sword wildly and aimlessly to the left, and to the right, while huffing and puffing as hard as he ever could to fend them all at once, "ERH! AAH! ERH! AAH! ERH! AAH! ERH! AAH . . . !"

After exhausting the entire battery unit of the plasma repeater Raven stopped firing and exclaimed, "Damn! I'm outta ammo!"

Thereafter, she strapped the weapon on her back and sensed that something was missing from their teamwork. She then realized that Keegan wasn't doing anything.

"Keegan!"

"Yes Raven?"

"Shoot! Shoot! They're coming!"

"I . . . I can't!"

As Keegan was about to explain, Raven continued shouting at him, "SHOOT! JUST SHOOT! ERGH!"

When Keegan continued refusing to fire, Raven became so annoyed yet stressed with the current situation that she shouted at him, "Keegan, you're just SHIT!"

Offended by Raven's words, Keegan angrily and forcefully shouted back, "YES! You're right! I'm just . . ." when he shouted the next word, which was "SHIT!", he farted with some noise, but was only slightly heard by Dusk. After which, he continued, "Okay? That's what I am!"

When Raven turned back, she saw that the ants had already gotten so close that she quickly shut her eyes and screamed in excruciating fear, "AAARRRGGGHHH!"

Feeling helpless, Keegan quickly faced down, shut his eyes, and braced for the end of his life. But then suddenly, all the ants unexpectedly stopped moving and stood still, as though time had stopped.

As soon as Dusk had decapitated the last ant, cold silence abruptly dominated the surrounding ambience. Nonetheless, he continued maintaining in high alert stance with his sword always ready. Surprised yet confused, he looked at all the other ants and mumbled to himself, "What?"

Upon hearing the sudden silence, Keegan thought he was already dead. Nonetheless, he slowly opened his eyes and to his greatest astonishment, he realized he was still alive. When he looked up, he saw his two other friends still standing by his sides, but were already surrounded by a massive swarm of ants. He then looked at the swarm and quickly realized that all the ants were not moving at all. Confused, he thought time had really stopped, and ended up staring blankly at everything around him, including the hexagonal tessellations of the stasis shield directly above him.

"What? But how . . ." mumbled Keegan.

When Raven experienced the same thing, she slowly opened her eyes, curious to know what had happened. But as soon as she did that, she saw how close the ants ahead of her were and in great fear, she immediately panicked, made a short sharp scream, and shut her eyes again. As the silence prevailed, and nothing still seemed to be happening, she began to sense something fishy about the situation. As such, she slowly opened her eyes once again. To her greatest shock, she saw that she and her friends had been surrounded by a massive swarm of frozen ants.

"Whoa . . ." awed Raven.

Suddenly, the swarm started moving once again. Immediately, Dusk brought his sword closer to his face in preparation for another slicing frenzy, while Raven panicked once more and screamed in terror, "AAARRRGGGHHH!"

Keegan quickly exclaimed, "HOLY!" and ducked his head with his eyes shut.

However, instead of going after the trio, the ants turned back and crawled away quickly. As Dusk was the only one witnessing this, he exclaimed, "They're . . . they're finally getting away! Guys! They're getting away! Oh thank goodness!"

Keegan and Raven heard what Dusk just said, and slowly opened their eyes. To their greatest relief, the ants were finally crawling back to where they came from.

When the last ant had disappeared from sight, Raven heaved a sigh of relief, "Ooh . . . thank goodness . . . thank goodness they're gone! I thought I'm already dead!"

"They've probably retreated! Good work Raven!" exclaimed Dusk.

"You too . . . thankfully, thankfully you're not like Keegan. Otherwise, we'd be dead already."

"Hey! Why did you say that? Don't you say anything bad about Keegan! What he did was actually right. I think he was the one who saved us!"

"Oh! Yeah? How?"

"Keegan! Explain."

As Keegan was still bearing a grudge against Raven, he kept quiet for some time before saying, "I just didn't shoot, okay? Because THEY'RE TOO CLOSE TO US! Unless you wanna die from the explosion!"

"Whoa! There's no need to shout. Remember where we are." said Dusk.

"Oh . . . sorry."

"It's okay, I understand how you feel. But after that, while Raven was saying something bad to you, I be wrong about this but . . . you . . . you farted . . . right?"

Shocked, Raven intervened, "What? Keegan you farted?"

"Quiet, let him speak." said Dusk.

When Raven kept quiet, Keegan gave Dusk and silent stare, and mumbled, "Fart? Are you serious?"

"Yeah, I heard it; well . . . it was pretty loud. You were probably too busy shouting to notice it."

"Oh . . . really?"

"Yeah!"

"Why're you asking me such questions? Can you stop being weird?"

"Then what do you think caused the ants to freeze, then scurry away? Hmm?"

After brainstorming for some time, Keegan realized that his fart was the most plausible cause.

"Hold on, was it because of my . . . fart?"

"Exactly! You finally got the point!"

"Oh I see!"

"Excellent job Keegan!"

"Haha! Thank you Dusk!"

While hearing the conversation between Dusk and Keegan, Raven realized that the way how she treated Keegan earlier was wrong. As she was about to apologize, awkward and disturbing noises sounded from all directions, "EEEKKK! EAOUARGH! ERAOURAH! ERHAGHA . . . !"

Suddenly, the swarm of ants reemerged from their colonies and quickly began crawling back towards the trio. When Dusk saw them coming, he quickly exclaimed, "Oh man! Keegan! Hurry! Do it!"

"The rocket pistol?"

"No! Fart! Now!"

"I can't! No more gas!"

"Raven! Howboutchiu!"

As Raven hasn't visited the toilet for the past two days, she felt slightly bloated and exclaimed, "I DO!"

Immediately, she applied force and farted, but this time, it was silent (silent and deadly). Dusk, who did not manage to hear anything exclaimed, "Are you done?"

"Yeah!"

"Great! Now hold your breath!"

The trio held their breath and endured the smell, patiently waiting to see if there would be any effect on the ants, although they were getting closer. When the smell reached the first ant, it suddenly stopped crawling and froze for a second. Meanwhile, it quickly scurried back into its colony, causing the rest to follow.

Hydrogen sulphide (fart gas) was an extreme irritant to the insects on Amiros.

When the trio realized that their plan was a great success, they heaved another sigh of relief.

"WHOA! It worked! Well done Raven, although I didn't hear anything." exclaimed Dusk.

Feeling contented, she thanked back with a smile, "Thanks!"

Dusk then caught sight of a PDA nearby, and called out to Keegan while pointing at it, "Keegan! Is that yours?"

Keegan looked at where Dusk had pointed, saw his gadget and exclaimed, "PDA? Ah! Yes!"

"Great! Could you still recall your plan you had for us earlier? What's the next step?"

Keegan pondered for some time, "Erm . . ." and finally exclaimed, "Yes! If I'm not wrong, I was pulled down here when I was about to convert the data of a Dreamstick from my PDA to its physical form!"

"Seems like you remembered! Great! Could you do that again?"

"Yeah, sure!"

"Excellent! But you gotta hurry. We don't have much time left. Remember, we're still in the stasis shield you created!"

"Oh! Okay, okay!"

Keegan reached for his PDA and managed to retrieve it without a hitch. Quickly, he accessed the "Storage" application and selected a long dreamstick, so as to accommodate the trio. A holographic model of the flying device was then projected ahead of his mobile device.

Thereafter, he gradually moved the hologram to a particular spot on the ground and it turned green, indicating that can be placed. When ready, he tapped "Place object" and immediately, transparent and highly refractive hexagonal tessellations began appearing with buzzing sounds on where he had pointed, bearing the shape of the dreamstick.

Fortunately, the entire conversion process was a success. The dreamstick became dynamic and fell to the ground due to the pull of gravity.

"Okay! Hop on! Quick!" exclaimed Dusk.

Quickly, the trio ran towards the dreamstick and activated it by flipping a switch by its side. When it had gradually ascended vertically to about waist level, Dusk raised one leg over it, and sat on it, like riding a horse, followed by Raven behind him.

"Hey! Gimmie a hand! It still hurts!" exclaimed Keegan.

"Alright! Let's get closer to him!" exclaimed Dusk.

Dusk, together with Raven sitting behind maneuvered the dreamstick and stopped just right next to Keegan. Raven then stretched one of her arms out to assist Keegan in getting up, but he refused, due to the grudge he still had against her.

"Come on Keegan! We don't have much time left!" exclaimed Raven.

"Keegan! I know how you feel. We shouldn't let such things be the end of us here. What's over is over! Come on! Get up! We gotta get outta here now, fast!"

After pondering for a few seconds, Keegan finally let the matter go and grabbed Raven's arm.

"Now that's the way! Come on Keegan! I've got you! The more it goes. Come on I've got you!"

Suddenly, the ants swarmed out from their colonies once more in their pursuit for the trio. But this time, they were all covered in a layer of gooish substance, which makes them immume to irritation from fart odor.

"Crap! They're coming back for us!" exclaimed Dusk.

"You hear that? Pull yourself up! Come on!" exclaimed Raven in rising anxiety.

Aware that the swarm had returned, Keegan panicked and pulled so hard that Raven felt strained and almost lost her balance.

"ARGH! That hurts! Stop pulling so hard! Come on! Use your other leg! You're not that heavy!"

Keegan used his other leg to push himself up while still enduring the stinging pain. This time, he finally made it, and quickly raised his wounded leg over the dreamstick.

"Great! Now your other leg! QUICK!"

Quickly, Keegan grabbed the dreamstick with his other arm, sat on it, and brought his other leg up. When ready, he released his grip from Raven, and tightly grabbed onto the dreamstick with both hands.

"GO!" exclaimed Keegan.

Immediately, the trio leaned forward, and the dreamstick abruptly accelerated. At the same time, Dusk pulled its front tip upwards and began ascending back into the stasis sphere above, which would be diminishing very soon.

When they had finally ascended to about a metre high, Raven looked down and exclaimed in great elation, as the swarm filled the space where the trio were trapped, "Whoa! We did it! Yeah!"

Dusk and Keegan then did the same and exclaimed in ultimate relief, "WHHOOAA!"

"Excellent work guys! Now we need to get as high as possible to avoid the creatures outside!" exclaimed Dusk.

"Don't forget what you did to them too!" exclaimed Raven.

"Oh yes! The flames!"

As the top interior surface of the stasis shield drew closer, Keegan exclaimed, "Careful guys! Don't fly over the boundary! It'll rip us apart!"

Surprised, Dusk exclaimed, "Oh, well said Keegan! At least you remembered what I told you!"

With his hands, Dusk applied force at the front end of the dreamstick, changing its direction till it began flying parallel to the inner surface of the stasis shield.

At this point, the trio were already flying at about 8 metres above the ground, high enough to avoid the heat and the plant creatures outside.

Meanwhile, the hexagonally tesselated membrane of the stasis shield gradually became fainter and fainter, while the fires outside began getting brighter and brighter as the plant creatures began moving faster and faster.

"Alright! You see that? The shield's gonna vanish at any moment now! Get ready!" exclaimed Dusk.

Keegan and Raven readied themselves for the moment of truth.

Dusk then began counting down, "Alright! On my count in three! Two! ONE! PULL! PULL! PULL . . . !"

When the stasis shield disappeared, all the plant creatures around, including the gigantic tarantula were suddenly engulfed in blazing flames, while being pushed back by invisible forces.

"EEAAOOU!" sounded the plant creatures in unparalleled pain as they were burnt alive.

Eventually, they ended up crashing to a single point, causing the flames to combine and form a massive inferno. It raged and burned like a furnace, generating smoke and incinerating anything and everything it touched, including nearby dormant trees.

"Oh . . . hot! Hot!" exclaimed Raven in great discomfort.

"I know you're hot Raven! Just hang in there!"

Getting the wrong idea, Raven kept silent.

Keegan endured the heat and continued grabbing tightly onto the dreamstick as Dusk comtinued ascending as fast as he could.

When the trio had ascended high enough, where the temperature was much cooler, they looked down and was completely astonished by what they saw.

"WWHHOOAA . . ."

Raven heaved another sigh of relief, and exclaimed, "We did it! Oh thank goodness we did it."

The trio flew through the thick and dense canopy above, and back into the clear skies where the bright lights of Ektha became visible once again.

"WHOO! Yeah! Well done guys! Really! Next stop, the mountain."

"Let's go!" exclaimed Keegan enthusiastically.

"I hope they're already there for us!" exclaimed Raven.

Keegan replied, "Well, they should be!"

"Let's hurry! We shouldn't keep them waiting!" exclaimed Dusk.

Suddenly, buzzing sounds, together with highly refractive tessellations of hexagonal cells began appearing on all the surfaces of the trio's bodies, including the dreamstick they were riding on.

Upon the sight of this, Raven astonishingly exclaimed, "WHOA What's . . . what's happening?"

Aware of what was happening, Dusk calmly answered, "Chill! You'll figure it out soon!"

In the next moment, the trio gradually expanded and returned to their original sizes.

CHAPTER 10

THE RAGING BIRD

Having escaped from the land of chaos, Dusk, Keegan and Raven continued their venture to the top of the highest mountain. They thought they had already made it until suddenly, something gargantuan pummeled upwards through the thick canopies below.

Hearing some noises from behind, and curious to know what it was, Keegan and Raven glanced back and were immediately stunned by what they saw—a gargantuan roc, which was so huge that its wings spanned over 30 metres wide.

"WHOA! Incoming!" exclaimed Keegan.

"What is it?" exclaimed Dusk while still looking straight.

"Oh my God! It's HUGE!" exclaimed Raven.

"Well it looks like a giant eagle!" exclaimed Keegan.

"What? Are you serious?" exclaimed Dusk in surprise.

"YES! And I have a bad feeling about this! It seems to be coming for us!"

During its pursuit for the trio, the roc made a deafening and high pitched shilling sound, similar to that of an eagle, "KREEEE . . . !"

Upon hearing it, Dusk exclaimed in agony, "Shrap! We need to speed up! Come on! Lean all the way forward!"

Keegan and Raven leaned forward as much as they could, but to their dismay, their efforts were to no avail. The roc was still catching up very quickly. Upon realizing this, Keegan anxiously exclaimed in great anguish while looking back, "IT'S GETTING CLOSER!"

Dusk exclaimed, "HOLD ON!" and forcefully pushed the dreamstick to one side. At the moment when the creature reached the trio, its claws whipped past them in a flash by just a mere centimeter. But then, its massive wings violently hit the back of the dreamstick, inflicting great damage to its chronium engines. Immediately Dusk lost control and began flying uncontrollably while leaving a trail of black smoke behind.

"WHOA, WHOA, WHOA, WHOA, WHOA . . . !" exclaimed the trio in terror.

"GUYS! I'VE LOST CONTROL! BRACE FOR IMPACT!" exclaimed Dusk.

Raven panicked and wailed, "Ohhh . . . we were so close to getting there! Tell me this isn't happening!"

Keegan continued grabbing tightly onto the dreamstick with his eyes shut.

"JUST HANG IN THERE!" exclaimed Dusk.

As the trio began descending lower and lower, the roc made a U turn, swiftly glided down through the air, and continued its pursuit for the trio while making high pitched shrilling sounds, "KREEEE . . . KREEEE . . . KREEEE . . . !"

But before reaching them, the trio pummeled through the thick canopy of the forest beneath. Immediately, the roc quickly flew back up to avoid hitting a large tree nearby.

Back within the canopy, the trio crash landed so forcefully against the mountainous surface that they literally smashed through everything that got in their way. Fortunately, they were just bushes and luminous epiphytes. When they had come to a complete stop, the trio fell to the ground and wailed in excruciating pain, "AARRGGHH! EERRGGHH!"

Keegan and Raven sustained deep cuts along their lower limbs, as well as some bone fractures. The same also happened to Dusk, but not as severe as his two other friends due to his immunity to physical impacts, which he secretly obtained in a research lab in Telrux University when he could no longer stand being bullied. Nonetheless, he still felt pain and wailed, "Argh!"

Meanwhile, he slowly looked back and shouted, "KEEGAN! RAVEN! YOU OKAY?"

While Keegan was still wailing in great pain, he raised his right hand and made an "Okay" sign with his fingers.

"Raven! Howboutchiu!" exclaimed Dusk.

"ERGH! DO I LOOK LIKE I'M OKAY?" exclaimed Raven while grabbing tightly onto her thighs with her hands while suffering in extreme pain.

At this point, everything (plants, vines and bushes) around the trio began moving once again, due to the noises and disturbances they had made. When Dusk saw this, he whined, "Oh . . . not again . . ."

Suddenly, something enormous pummeled through the thick canopy above, smashing through every branch and vegetation in its way like a meteor, and landed with a very loud thud. The ground shuddered as though an earthquake had struck, shaking everything nearby. To the trio's greatest surprise, the thing turned out to be the same roc that had been chasing them earlier. Immediately, all the plant creatures surrounding the trio quickly scurried off, as they feared rocs due to their ferociousness and immense size.

"KREEEE . . . !"

Upon seeing this, Dusk exclaimed in his greatest anxiety, "HOLY SHI . . . IT! QUICK! GET UP! DO SOMETHING!"

When Keegan and Raven saw the roc, they widened their eyes, but could do nothing due to their intolerable pains in their wounds. As such, they continued wailing on the ground.

Dusk quickly took his PDA out in the attempt to hijack the conscious mind of the roc, just like what he did to a tarantula earlier.

"Come on . . . Come on!" mumbled Dusk to himself as he quickly accessed the "Consciousness manipulator" application and selected the "Hijack" option. Thereafter, he quickly pointed the tip of his mobile device at the raging bird. However, as he was on the brink of hitting the activation button; the roc forcefully swung one of its massive wings and hit his entire arm that was holding onto the mobile device. The force was so potent that he somersaulted through the air and landed on his chest. His PDA flew into the bushes in the distance, and became barely visible due to its small size.

In great pain, Dusk wailed, "AAOOWWEERRH! MAN! I WAS SO CLOSE! AARRGGHH!"

"KREEEE . . . KREEEE . . . KREEEE . . . !" shrilled the roc.

When Dusk had recovered from the pain, he quickly got up and scoured the area for his PDA. However, he looked back and saw that the raging creature was already approaching Keegan and Raven.

"NO! DON'T YOU DARE!" exclaimed Dusk angrily.

Aware that it would be too late by the time he had found his PDA, he quickly welded his Danium Sword to his right arm and activated its energy blades.

"TTSSHH . . . !"

Immediately, the roc stopped moving and sensed the sound as a threat. In the next moment, it diverted its attention towards Dusk by turning and stomping forcefully against the ground, "THUNG, THUNG, THUNG!"

"KREEEE . . . KREEEE . . . !" shrilled the roc.

When the two were finally facing each other head on, Dusk angrily stared at the raging bird, while holding his Danium Sword on his right arm.

"Alright you little bird . . . you've asked for it . . . you wanna fight? Come on . . . come on now . . ."

It appeared as though a duel between a young boy and a roc had begun. When ready, Dusk slowly took small steps forward with the intention to punch his sword through the roc's throat when within reach, just like what he did to the ants.

"That's it . . . come on . . . come on . . . you'll get it . . . that's it . . ."

The roc slowly began approaching Dusk, but also being extra cautious at the same time.

"KREEEE . . . KREEEE . . . !" shrilled the roc.

But before Dusk could even get close enough to do anything, the roc forcefully swung one of its wings and hit him in the face, throwing him afar. But luckily, he managed to react in time by raising his sword, which flew from his hand and sliced through the wing of the roc. It then landed into a nearby river of fast flowing water, causing it to boil quickly and cook every aquatic life in it to death.

In great pain, the roc shook itself erratically and jumped around while shrilling loudly, "KREEEE . . . KREEEE . . . KHREEEE . . . !"

Dusk forcefully landed onto the ground and rolled for some distance before coming to a stop. In great pain, he wailed, "AARRGGHH . . . ! CRAP! EERRGGHH!"

Meanwhile, the roc quickly approached Dusk in the attempt to stomp him to death despite the wound in its wing.

"KHEEAA . . . KHEEAAH . . . !" shrilled the roc.

Dusk opened his eyes and saw the raging bird dashing towards him. With no PDA, weapon or whatsoever, he felt a sense of helplessness, closed his eyes and bracing for death.

"Oh god, no . . . o!" exclaimed Dusk in helplessness and fear.

Suddenly, he heard a massive explosion coming from the roc. "BHOOM . . . !"

Thereafter, he heard the roc shrilling very loudly, as though it was suffering in excruciating pain, "KHEEAA . . . KHEEAA . . . KHEEAAH . . . !"

Curious to know what had happened, he slowly opened his eyes and to his greatest shock, the roc was dashing around while leaving behind a trail of blue flames coming from its tail.

Relieved, he realized that Keegan had finally used the rocket pistol which he had passed to him earlier and exclaimed, "THANK YOU KEEGAN! THANK YOU! EXCELLENT WORK WITH THAT PISTOL! OH! THANK YOU!"

Unfortunately, the roc managed to extinguish the fire and endure the pain. Thereafter, it began dashing towards Keegan to finish him off. Shocked to see the roc coming, Keegan screamed in unparalleled fear with his eyes shut, as he had fired his one and only rocket, "WHAT? No . . . It's coming . . . no . . . NO . . . O!"

"AAARRRGGGHHH!" screamed Raven as she quickly shut her eyes.

Unable to bear witnessing the end of his two friends, Dusk closed his eyes and prayed, "Oh God . . . this can't be happening . . . I . . . I must be dreaming . . . wake up . . . wake up . . . WAKE UP!"

CHAPTER 11

THE MYSTERIOUS BIRD

When the roc was on the brink of reaching them, another bird emerged from deep within the forest, shrilling, "KHEA! KHEA! KHEA!"

It flew past the roc's head and popped its left eye with its sharp beak.

In excruciating pain, the roc landed its feet just right next to Keegan when it stopped, and wailed while swaying its head randomly in all directions, "KKHHIIAA . . . KKHHIIAA . . . KKHHIIAA . . . !"

When the trio heard this, they slowly opened their eyes and saw another bird-like creature flying above them. To their greatest astonishment, it turned out to be a resplendent flaming blue phoenix, a mysterious bird that leaves trails of blue flames behind as it flew.

The blue phoenix then made a U-turn ahead, and flew back to the roc. This time, it flew past the other side of its head and popped its other eye, rendering it completely blind.

"KKHHIIAA . . . KKHHIIAA . . . KKKHHHIIIAAA . . . !"

At this point, the trio was just sitting ducks, unable to do anything but just watch the fight between the two legendary birds.

The blue phoenix continued harassing the roc by pinching its body with its beak while flying around it. No longer able to tolerate the pain and harassment, the roc quickly opened its wings and took off. Immediately, the blue phoenix gave chase.

As the roc has been visually impaired, it blindly flew into a gigantic cobweb above and got stuck in it.

"KKHHIIA . . . KKHHIIAA . . . !" wailed the roc as it struggled in the cobweb.

Upon seeing this, the blue phoenix turned back and began flying towards Keegan and Raven. When Dusk saw this, he closed his eyes once again, unable to bear the sight of what could possibly happen next.

When Keegan and Raven saw the beautiful and mysterious bird flying closer towards them, they silently shut their eyes and braced for the end of their lives. Meanwhile, they felt a sudden tremor and heard a loud thud right next to them.

Keegan prayed softly to himself, hoping that the phoenix would not kill anyone, "Oh God please no . . . no . . . please no . . . oh God . . . please . . ."

After which, there was a moment of silence, a moment where the trio had prepared and expected for what was to come—death.

But after praying for about a minute, nothing still seemed to be happening. So, Keegan thought, "Am I dead?"

Curious to know, he slowly opened his eyes and the first thing he saw right in front of his face was the gleaming head of the blue phoenix, which was sticking from the left and facing to the right. It had resplendent blue and fiery eyes and was covered in bright blue feathers. Overwhelmed by how beautiful it was, he yelped, "WHOA!" and fell backwards.

Meanwhile, the blue phoenix winked an eye at Keegan. Shocked by the intelligence of the creature, Keegan couldn't believe what he just saw and continued staring at it.

Then suddenly, the blue phoenix spoke softly with a bird-like voice, "Quick . . . come with me if you wanna live. Get yourself and your friends on me. We need to get outta here fast."

Couldn't believe what he just heard, Keegan became so overwhelmed with extreme astonishment that his eyes immediately widened as his jaws dropped.

When Raven heard the same thing, she gradually opened her eyes and was stunned to see how close the blue phoenix was to

Keegan. Immediately, she had the same reaction as Keegan, but managed to stay silent to avoid provoking the mysterious bird.

As Dusk was relatively far away, about 20 metres from his two other friends, he did not manage to hear the voice of the phoenix. So, unaware of anything happening, he continued shutting his eyes with his hands over his head.

Meanwhile, Keegan timidly replied the blue phoenix, "Who . . . who are you?"

The blue phoenix answered, "You'll know that later. Quick, hop on me! Now!"

Keegan turned back and said to Raven, "Should we?"

Raven pondered for some time and answered, "But . . . how can you trust it?"

"I dunno, it just sounds like it really wants to help us."

"Really?"

"Er . . ."

Suddenly, the blue phoenix continued, "Do you trust me?"

Unable to give an answer, Keegan and Raven kept silent.

"Fine, have it your way." said the blue phoenix.

Judging by the way how the blue phoenix spoke, Raven remembered about Dusk, for that was coincidentally what he said to her when she refused to lend her PDA to him. She then looked around in the search for him and saw him squatting with his hands over his head at some distance away. She then stared at Keegan and said, "How about Dusk?"

"Oh, he's still there? Don't call him. It'll attract unnecessary attention, especially when the roc isn't here anymore. Perhaps this phoenix could do some help in this."

"Alright . . ."

Keegan looked into the eyes of the blue phoenix and asked, "Would you mind doing for us a little favor?"

"What is it?" said the blue phoenix.

"To also save our friend right there, he seems traumatized."

The blue phoenix looked afar, saw Dusk in the distance and replied, "Okay . . . quick, hop onto my back first."

When the blue phoenix lowered itself, Keegan slowly got up while enduring the great pain in his legs, "AARRGGHH!"

"You okay?" exclaimed Raven.

"Yeah! Just a little more . . . ARGH!"

Keegan made it and finally stood on his feet. Thereafter, he said to Raven, "Need a hand?"

"Yeah."

"Here! Come on!" said Keegan as he stretched one of his arm towards Raven to help her up. Touched by Keegan, Raven learnt a lesson on forgiveness and quickly grabbed his arms.

"That's the way. Come on Raven, you can do it! Pull yourself up! Come on!"

"AARRGGHH!" wailed Raven while attempting to stand.

"You got it! Come on, get on! Be careful!"

When the two had safely sat onto the back of the blue phoenix, Keegan patted its back three times to indicate that they were ready. The blue phoenix then stood on its feet and cautiously made its way towards Dusk, while making as little noise as possible.

When Dusk heard the crushing sounds of dried leaves approaching him, he thought his friends were already dead, and he was the next victim. As such, he remained still like a statue.

The blue phoenix stopped just right in front of Dusk and said to him, "Wakie wakie!"

Stunned by what he just heard, and curious to know what it was, he slowly opened his eyes and saw the gleaming head of the blue phoenix just directly in front of his face.

Immediately, he shockfully yelled to the top of his lungs with his eyes wide opened and fell backwards. His reaction was so intense that it appeared as though he had just won a trillion dollars, "WWHHOOAA . . . HOLY SHRAP!"

Dusk's yell was so loud and deafening that the blue phoenix quickly shut its eyes and took a step backwards. But unfortunately, he had also unintentionally attracted the attention of all the plant creatures around him.

When Dusk became aware that what he had just done was so wrong, he fearfully observed his surroundings and saw everything (bushes, vines and epiphytes) around him moving once more. He then fearfully looked into the eyes of the blue phoenix with a racing heartbeat, thinking that it wanted to kill him. Hence, he began crawling backwards in sitting position till he saw Keegan and Raven on its back.

"What? Keegan? Raven?" mumbled Dusk in great confusion and surprise at the same time.

"Dusk!" exclaimed Raven. "You gotta hop on with us! This bird's bargin' us outta here! Come on!"

Dusk became more confident that the blue phoenix was harmless, and stopped crawling, but still maintained his stare at it.

When the blue phoenix slowly brought its head closer towards Dusk by stretching its neck forward, he panicked slightly by breathing more rapidly due to its huge size.

The blue phoenix then spoke to Dusk, "Listen, we have to go now. Everything here is already coming for us. Quick, grab your PDA and climb onto my neck, I'll slide you to my back by raising it. Hurry!"

"Oh . . . okay!"

When Dusk stood up to search for his PDA, the blue phoenix said to him, "Your PDA's just right behind that bush!" and pointed its head to the direction where it had landed. Fortunately, the bush was dormant, as not all the plants around were moving.

Dusk saw the bush, quickly ran over with great caution, picked it up, kept it, and then ran back.

At this point, some of the plant creatures around began making weird and eerie noises, "EEAAOOWW HOOH!", and were set free from the soil they were bound to. They then quickly picked up speed in their pursuit of the blue phoenix by crawling rapidly across the sandy ground.

When Keegan and Raven saw them coming, they quickly exclaimed to Dusk in great anticipation, "DUSK! THEY'RE COMING! HURRY!"

CHAPTER 12

ONE FINAL EFFORT

When Dusk heard his friends, he quickened his pace while looking back to ensure he wasn't chased by anything. When he reached the blue phoenix, he quickly jumped onto its neck and shouted, "OKAY! GO, GO, GO!"

Immediately, the blue phoenix raised its neck, slid Dusk down to its cool yet burning back, and began sprinting forward as fast as it could.

"You okay?" said Raven.

Dusk looked into Raven's eyes and exhaustedly answered while nodded his head, "Hyeah!"

Eventually, a massive hoard of plant creatures clustered at the back, frantically chasing the trio on the blue phoenix. Upon looking back, Dusk exclaimed in shock, "Whoa! We'd be dead already if it weren't for this bird!"

"Yeah!" exclaimed Keegan.

"I wonder where it came from!"

"I dunno! For now, just HANG IN THERE!"

In the next moment, the blue phoenix jumped, opened its beautiful blue burning wings, and went airborne.

"WHOA! It's flying!" exclaimed Dusk in great relief.

Nonetheless, it did not fly very high, as there were full of cobwebs above. Rather, it flew only to increase its speed while saving more energy. To the trio's greatest surprise, the blue phoenix was flying in the correct direction, which was the highest point of the mountain.

"It's . . . its flying the right way! YEAH!" exclaimed Dusk elatedly.

When the blue phoenix had reached the summit, it flew into a plain grassland, where there were six legged reptilian goats grazing on the grasses, and no longer anymore thick vegetation. While flying through, the blue phoenix scared all the reptilian goats off as they scurry away, while plant creatures were still chasing from behind.

This time, the trio looked ahead and finally saw something they had been longing to see—a rescue dropship, which was already positioning its back ramp access door to the edge of a cliff at only about two hundred metres ahead.

"OH! I SEE IT! THAT'S THE DROPSHIP!" exclaimed Raven in ultimate relief.

"YES! WE MADE IT!" exclaimed Keegan in the same way.

"COME ON! FLOOR IT! RIGHT INTO THE HANGAR!" shouted Dusk in great anticipation and anxiety as the blue phoenix flapped its wings even harder and sped up.

But as they were just about to enter the rescue dropship, a massive and ferocious three-headed hydra launched upwards from the water body beneath and devoured the spacecraft with its gigantic jaws. Immediately, the dropship was crushed and exploded violently in blue flames, ricocheting glass fragments and metal debris everywhere.

Upon seeing this, the hearts of the trio melted, and they cried, "NOOOO . . . O!"

Quickly, the blue phoenix dodged by changing its direction of flight. When it began flying straight once more, the trio looked ahead and saw another rescue dropship ahead, this time hovering just above the grassy surface. In great relief, Keegan exclaimed, "OH! THANK GOODNESS THEY SENT ANOTHER DROPSHIP!"

"GogogogogoGOGO!" exclaimed Dusk in great anticipation.

But unfortunately, the second dropship was already closing its back ramp access door and going on full throttle to escape the planet, possibly due to the destruction of the first. When Dusk saw this happening, he exclaimed in agony, "WHAT? WHY'RE THEY LEAVING WITHOUT US? COME ON! WE STILL HAVE A CHANCE! FLOOR IT! GO . . . O!"

Upon hearing what Dusk had shouted, the blue phoenix expended all its energy by mightily swaying its wings forwards and backwards. It then began flying at lightning speed, faster than a racecar in the risky attempt to enter the hangar at the back of the dropship without being crushed by its ramp access door.

As the gap between the top of the ramp and the ceiling got smaller, Dusk continuously shouted in great anticipation, hoping the best he ever could that the blue phoenix would make it through successfully, "AAAARRRRGGGGHHHH . . . !"

At this point, Keegan and Raven quickly shut their eyes and braced for the unexpected.

By the time the ramp access door had reached its halfway point to closing, the phoenix streamlined its body till it was as flat as a disc. Fortunately, it made it past the raising ramp and violently crashed into the hangar, throwing the trio forward through the air, like rocks being launched from a catapult.

"ARGH . . . H!" exclaimed the trio as they were thrown.

Keegan and Raven smashed against a wall ahead, while Dusk collided against a weapons compartment. Due to the great force, it broke from the wall, fell to the ground, and was smashed open, revealing several M173 Needle sniper rifles, as well as some other weapons, such as pistols and assault rifles inside.

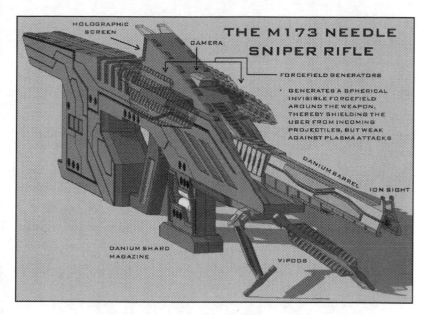

A sketch of the M173 Needle sniper rifle of Hexiron
with upgraded barrel for danium and rail rounds

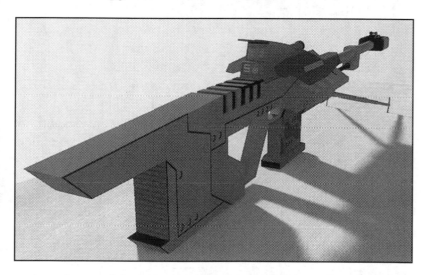

A rendering of the M173 Needle sniper rifle of Hexiron without
the upgraded barrel, depicting its on-screen displays. The top
screen displays the digital scope for aiming, while the bottom
one displays a compass and the number of rounds remaining

"AARRGGHH . . . HUGH . . . AAHH!" wailed Dusk in great pain in the chest, and Keegan and Raven in the limbs.

The blue phoenix came to a complete stop rather quickly before hitting the wall ahead due to its great surface area and friction against the rough ground. From there, it became motionless due to over exhaustion.

Unfortunately, as the plant creatures behind were also catching up very quickly, one pear-shaped plant-like creature took a leap forward in the attempt to enter the hangar. But by the time it had reached the ramp access door, the gap was already too small that it got clamped between the ceiling and the top part of the ramp, with its ravenous mouth and sharp teeth facing directly at the trio, who were already severely injured from the crash earlier.

Shocked by the sudden appearance of the plant-like creature, the trio quickly turned their heads and stared at its ravenous gnashing teeth. The creature also seemed to be squeezing its way into the hangar by pushing itself forward with its vines and roots.

"OH MY GOD!" exclaimed Raven in absolute shock. "DO SOMETHING!"

Too painful to do anything else, the trio did not manage to do anything. When Keegan remembered that he still had one freezenade, he quickly unstrapped it from his belt and quickly pulled the safety pin off. He then brought the freezenade to the back of his head, took aim and exclaimed, "EAT THIS!"

Without delay, he forcefully threw the freezenade and to everyone's surprise, it flew directly into the mouth of the plant-like creature, and it swallowed it.

For a moment, its mouth was closed, and nothing seemed to be happening, so, it reopened its mouth and continued gnashing its teeth while making loud eerie noises, "EEEAAAOOOWWW! EEAAHH!"

Suddenly, an explosion sounded from the inside of the plant creature, "PTSHKKLLIIAANNGGSHHKLK . . . !"

Immediately, blue ice began appearing on all the surfaces of its body till it became fully covered in ice. After which, there was a moment of silence as the trio began staring at it.

In great pain, Keegan carefully dragged himself across the floor to a M173 Needle sniper rifle that had dropped onto the floor and grabbed a magazine of five rail rounds nearby. He then loaded it into the sniper rifle and cocked its charging handle, sending one bullet into the firing chamber, "CHI KLIAK!"

When ready, gradually held the sniper rifle upright, and began taking aim. When ready, he solemnly whispered to himself, "Hastalavista . . . baby . . ."

He pulled the trigger, "PSHKLING!"

Immediately, the plant-like creature literally shattered into countless pieces of ice fragments.

"PPPTSSSKKKLLLIIIAAANNNGGG . . . KANG!"

As soon as that happened, the ramp access door continued closing till it became fully shut.

With great exhaustion, Keegan released the sniper rifle from his hands and fell back down.

Suddenly, the blue phoenix, which was lying motionless ahead, began emanating weird buzzing sounds.

"BZAZAZAZAZAZA . . . !"

When Raven saw what was happening, she said softly to Dusk while lying on the ground like Keegan, "What . . . what's happening?"

Dusk, still in pain answered, "I . . . I don't know."

At this moment, the trio could do nothing, but observe something strange happening to the mysterious bird which saved them.

Meanwhile, transparent and highly refractive hexagonal tessellations began appearing on all the surfaces of the blue phoenix till it became completely transparent like glass. It then began shrinking while slowly shape-shifting into a small human, who was lying face-on against the floor.

CHAPTER 13

THE REVELATION

Mesmerized by what he just saw, Dusk mumbled to himself in confusion, "Wha . . . at?"

"Whoa . . ." Keegan and Raven as they continued staring.

"Who is that . . ." mumbled Raven.

No one answered.

When the tessellations of hexagonal cells began fading into physical form, Dusk strained his eyes and took a closer look at who the person is.

To everyone's greatest surprise, the small man turned out to be Dusk himself, literally transformed from a blue phoenix back to his original form. With unparalleled astonishment, Dusk immediately widened his eyes with his jaws dropped. He was so shocked to the extent that he froze and couldn't say a single word.

Keegan and Raven gave the same response and was rendered completely still.

When the transformation has been completed, Dusk's so called "clone" slowly stood up in great exhaustion and some pain. It then took a step forward and looked at the trio ahead. While taking deep breaths, it stretched an arm forward and said to them in a tired voice while coughing, "Don't worry . . . EHRGH! EHRGH!"

After a moment of silence, the "clone" of Dusk continued speaking while still taking deep breaths, "I . . . I'm Dusk. I . . . I was told by myself to go back in time to find and save you. Finally, it is finished!"

Upon hearing this, the trio was so shocked to the extent that they almost fainted. Thereafter, Dusk, who came from the future looked into the eyes of his past self, and began taking small steps towards him while saying, "Dusk . . . oh, I can't believe I'm talking to myself now."

Dusk from the present time stunningly answered, "Oh . . . you're, you're me in the future?"

"Yeah . . . which means that . . . there is something very important you've got to do now."

"What is it?"

"Everything that I've just done."

Stunned, Dusk from the present time bellowed, "What?"

"Heh . . . love how I respond. So, I need you to go back in time, alright?"

"Oh! So I guess this is now I ended up . . . speaking to myself?"

"Yes, I said that too before I turn the time. Now, listen . . . go back in time and transform yourself into a blue phoenix. Then find us and save us. You should roughly know where you and your friends should be at."

"Oh . . . and what if I don't do it?"

"I dunno . . . maybe you'll be crushed to bits just because you've violated the laws of nature? Better not try that. Somehow, you'll still have to go back in time and do what I just did. Don't worry, cuz success has been guaranteed. Look at who's speaking to you right now."

"Okay, so . . . how do I do it?"

"There's a "Time Turner" app in your PDA. Access it and enter the value "20" into "Number of minutes to turn". After that, do not activate the application yet. I repeat, do not activate the application yet. Can you understand that?"

"Yeah! go on . . ."

"Okay, after that, enter the "Morph into creature after turning time" option and select "Sparkle", your blue phoenix."

"Oh so it's my pet phoenix! No wonder it looked so familiar! No wonder the plant creatures weren't afraid of it! I thought it was one of the creatures on this planet!"

The future self of Dusk smiled and said, "Yup! Haha, no it isn't."

"I see!"

"After that, the moment of truth. Activate the app, and it'll bring you back in time by creating a copy of yourself as a blue phoenix at where you are right now. So you'll be appearing in midair, right here, at the instant after you activate the app. This means that you'll have to fly back to Droughalis and look for your past self and friends."

"Oooh . . . !"

"Are you ready?"

"Er . . . sort of . . ."

"You've gotta be brave alright? As blue phoenix, you should pull no chances to the roc."

"Okay."

Dusk from the present time nodded and took his PDA out. In the home page, he scrolled through the apps and accessed the "Time Turner" application with a touch of his finger.

Once inside, he did everything as instructed and before hitting the activation button, he looked up into the eyes of his future self and friends in silence.

Emotionally, he slowly and monotonously said his last words before going back in time, "Goodbye . . . but I'll be back. No matter what, we'll be friends forever . . . Just hang on . . . Just hang on . . ."

Feeling touched, tears began rolling down from Raven's eyes as she waved farewell to him, "Goodbye Dusk . . . I wish you all the best . . ."

"Good luck Dusk . . . I trust you . . ." said Keegan.

Thereafter, Dusk from the future placed his right hand on the left shoulder of his past self and confidently said, "Do you believe in yourself?"

Without delay, Dusk from the present time bravely answered, "YES!"

"Good! Then do it . . . good luck!"

The future self of Dusk then slowly released his hand from his past self, and his past self gradually moved his finger to the activation button on the holographic interface of his PDA. When it came into contact, the application got activated, and immediately, transparent and highly refractive hexagonal tessellations began appearing on all the surfaces of his body while emanating buzzing sounds, "BZAZAZAZAZAZA . . . ZAZA!"

While this was happening, Keegan, Raven, and the future self of Dusk kept their eyes locked at his past self as he was slowly disappearing, while creating a copy of himself as a blue phoenix back in time.

Eventually, he became clear as crystal and diminished into thin air. When nothing was left behind, Dusk quickly approached his two friends, knelt down, and hugged them with tears rolling down his eyes. With great emotions and appreciation for his friends, he whispered, "Thank you for everything . . . We wouldn't have made it if it weren't for us . . . I . . . I love you guys . . ."

The trio then cried, as they once again discover the true meaning of true friends and forgiving each other during tough times to overcome challenges, especially Keegan and Raven. With that, the friendship and bond between them strengthened further.

CHAPTER 14

POWER OF HEXIRON

Meanwhile, Dusk so happened to look up, and to his surprise, he saw something gargantuan appearing out of nowhere in the sky through the plasma windows of the hangar.

Stunned, he stared at the gigantic entity and softly mumbled to his friends, "Guys . . . something's appearing in the sky."

When Keegan and Raven turned back and looked into the direction where Dusk was looking, they saw the same massive entity, which quickly turned out to be an Aqrian battleship, which is a hostile alien race that has been haunting humans since their first invasion on Earth.

"WHAT? An Aqrian ship? Why're they even here?" exclaimed Raven in astonishment.

Dusk quickly answered, "Looks like we're not alone here after all!"

"You kidding me?" exclaimed Keegan.

"Why would I?"

In the next moment, the trio saw violet laser beams being fired from the extraterrestrial battleship towards them. Quickly, Dusk ducked down and exclaimed, "WHOA! GET DOWN!"

Without delay, Keegan and Raven ducked down for cover.

"Oh . . . I hope it doesn't hit us . . ." whispered Raven in doubt and fear, hoping that the rescue dropship would make it out unscathed.

Suddenly, they heard loud splashing sounds of water in the direction of the battleship. It sounded as tough a meteor shower had landed into the waters. The area was then lit up so brightly that rays of light were seen passing through the plasma windows of the hangar. As sound travels slower than light, the trio then heard another loud noise in the same direction, but this time, it was a massive and deafening explosion.

Curious to know what had happened, Dusk took a peep outside and was astonished to see that the hull of one side of the battleship had been severely and deeply scarred from top to bottom, just like Valles Marineris, which is a system of canyons on the surface of Mars. It appeared as though a large meteor had literally sliced past its side. When he continued observing, he saw several holes, together with raging flames and flying debris along the top hull of the battleship as it slowly began descending. Concluding that the ship has been destroyed, he shockingly exclaimed, "WHOA! It's . . . it's destroyed!"

Stunned, Keegan and Raven bellowed, "What?"

"But how?" exclaimed Keegan.

"It looks like it's been hit by a tungsten high velocity slug fired from a MAC in space." said Dusk.

The trio continued staring at the alien battleship as it fell into the vast ocean beneath in defeat, splashing waters as high as the Willis Tower in Chicago up in all directions.

When everything was over, Keegan and Raven lay back down and rested. Dusk stood up and began approaching the bridge of the rescue dropship, as the pilots may not be aware that he and his friends were already on board. When he reached the DFD that leads to the bridge, he saw two pilots behind and knocked against it.

"Kokokokokokokok!"

Surprised to hear the knocking sounds, the pilots looked back and were stunned to see Dusk standing outside.

"Who's that? How . . . how did he get in here?" said one of the pilots to the other.

"I dunno, but he should be one of the guys we should be rescuing."

"Oh . . ."

"Shall we let him in? Perhaps he has something to tell us."

"No! We already lost contact with Falcon 222! How can you trust that he's human?"

"What makes you say that?"

"We're in Amiros! Not Earth! If you wish to communicate with him, use the announcement system."

"Okay."

The pilot activated the announcement system and spoke, "This is Falcon 223. Identify yourself."

Dusk replied, "I'm . . . I'm Dusk, Dusk Cooper, a friend of Keegan who called you to rescue us."

"Oh . . . But, how did you manage to get on board?"

"Well . . . it's a very long story to tell."

CHAPTER 15

HOME SWEET HOME

The trio was finally escorted safely out of Amiros to a S557 Salvation Battleship stationed just outside the planet. This was the battleship that fired the MAC (magnetic accelerator cannon) rounds and eliminated the Aqrian threat on the alien planet earlier.

THE S-557 SALVATION, CLASS C
BATTLESHIP OF HEXIRON

Length: 1,800 m
Width: 296.13 m
Height: 161.85 m
Engine: Chromium Fusion Reactors
Hull: 60 cm Titanium
Armament: 8x Large Turret Slots
Roles: Protection of Larger Fleet Ships
Affiliation: Hexiron

DESIGN AND ARTWORK BY: JERVIS T.C.H.,
AUTHOR OF DUSK: DEATH ISLAND

Once docked, the battleship flew out of the star system of Ektha, and to the Acratum star system, where the parent star was surrounded by three artificial ringworlds. The ringworlds, with increasing distance from the parent star are known as Elysium Ringworlds A, B and C respectively.

THE ARTIFICIAL RINGWORLD SYSTEMS OF ACRATUM: ACRATIA

ACRATUM IS A SUN-LIKE STAR WITH A SPECTRAL TYPE OF F9V, AND IS LOCATED ABOUT 17,000 LIGHT-YEARS FROM EARTH IN THE CONSTELLATION MONOCEROS.

SURROUNDING THIS STAR IS A SUPERMASSIVE MEGASTRUCTURE CALLED ACRATIA, WHICH COMPRISE THREE 1,100,000 KM WIDE AND 200,000 KM THICK ARTIFICIALLY CONSTRUCTED HABITABLE RING SYSTEMS CALLED ELYSIUM RINGWORLDS, WHICH ARE LABELLED FROM A TO C WITH INCREASING DIAMETERS.

THEY ROTATE IN THE CLOCKWISE DIRECTION, THEREBY GENERATING CENTRIFUGAL GRAVITY EQUIVALENT TO THAT OF EARTH (1 g) ON THEIR INNER SURFACES. THEREFORE, IF YOU WERE TO LIVE ALONG ONE OF THE EDGES OF ELYSIUM RINGWORLD B, YOU WILL OCCASIONALLY SEE OTHER RINGWORLD SYSTEMS <u>PASSING DIRECTLY OVER</u> OR <u>UNDER</u> YOU. THE SIGHT IS EXTREMELY AND OVERWHELMINGLY MAGNIFICENT.

DAY AND NIGHT CYCLES ARE ALSO REGULATED ON THE RINGWORLDS BY THREE SEMICIRCULAR RINGS ORBITING THE STAR AT A CLOSER DISTANCE. THE OTHER HALF OF THESE RINGS ARE FULLY MADE OF A COMPLETELY TRANSPARENT MATERIAL TO ACHIEVE ORBITAL STABILITY

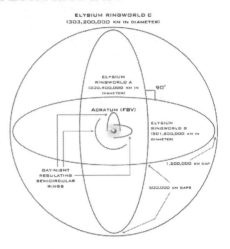

ELYSIUM RINGWORLD C (303,200,000 KM IN DIAMETER)

ELYSIUM RINGWORLD A (300,400,000 KM IN DIAMETER)

ACRATUM (F9V)

ELYSIUM RINGWORLD B (301,800,000 KM IN DIAMETER)

90°

1,200,000 KM GAP

DAY-NIGHT REGULATING SEMICIRCULAR RINGS

500,000 KM GAPS

The battleship flew to an offshore island along one of the edges of Elysium Ringworld B, where a prestigious school called Telrux University was located. Once reached, it hovered above the school for refueling, while the trio was transported to the medical facility at Rubicon, School of PDA Applications and Technologies in D38 SB Sabres, which are infantry carrier dropships. They were different from the rescue dropships used previously.

A rendering of a D38 SB Sabre of Hexiron

As the majestic University drew closer, Dusk looked through the plasma windows, down onto the ground and saw a group of four M98A3 Behemoths moving in the more remote area of the island.

The M98A3 Behemoth Superheavy Battle Tank of Hexiron

Surprised, he exclaimed, "Wow look! What're they doing down there?"

While sleeping on a medical rolling bed at the other side of the dropship, Raven was awakened and answered drowsily, "What?"

Keagan, who was sitting just right next to Raven answered, "What did you see?"

"Er . . . four very big tanks in the grass fields!"

"Oh! Our classmates must be practicing for the end of year games, which will be coming very soon!"

"OOH! I see! I didn't know they would bring such tanks in for the games, awesome!"

"Look forward to it?"

"Of course! And the two of you will be my teammates!"

"Yeah! That's the spirit Dusk! Do you think our school can count on us to win?"

"Definitely! I mean . . . look! We're already one of their best students!"

"So you'll be the game changer?"

"Absolutely!"

Too tired to say anything, all Raven could do was just smile and continued sleeping.

In the next moment, while the four superheavy tanks were still on the move, they rotated their main guns and aimed their turrets at four floating targets in the air (one per target). Thereafter, they began charging their weapons and before Dusk knew it, they fired destructive railguns, effectively destroying them in just two shots.

"PSHUNGKHLING! PSHUNGKHLING!" sounded the firing of the railguns.

Eventually, the D38 Sabre hovered above the medical facility and slowly descended onto a landing pad. There, trio were then brought to their wards with the help of several assistants and escorts, and were healed in just a few days with the help of healing applications from their doctors' PDAs.

MAP OF DROUGHALIS

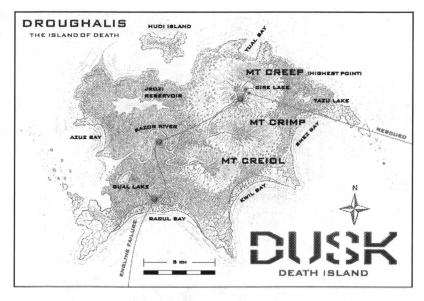

Droughalis is a small island located on the planet Amiros, which is an earth-like planet of Ektha, its parent star. Although it is small, it harbors a vast array of aberrant lifeforms.

The island has three mountains, namely Mount Creiol, Mount Crimp and Mount Creep. Out of the three, Mount Creep is the highest. It rises to a height of 4,758 feet above sea level and has a lake called Cire Lake at its summit. This lake can also be known as the lake of death due to the ravenous creatures, such as hydras lurking throughout its waters.

Green lines: Travelling with a flying vehicle
Red lines: Travelling without a flying vehicle
Blue lines: Travelling with the blue phoenix

DETAILS OF AMIROS

Orbital characteristics	
Apastron (farthest orbital distance from parent star)	123,567,841 km (0.826 AU)
Periastron (nearest orbital distance from parent star)	120,426,285 km (0.805 AU)
Semi-major axis	121,997,063 km (0.8155 AU)
Eccentricity	0.012876
Rotational period	46.7 Earth hours
Orbital period	338 Earth days
Average orbital speed	94,308 km/h
Inclination	1.264° relative to Ektha's equator
Satellites	2 natural moons (Amiros I and II)

Physical characteristics	
Equatorial radius	5,974.3 km
Polar Radius	5,863.5 km
Mean radius	5,918.9 km
Mean diameter	11,837.8 km
Equatorial circumference	37,189.55 km
Surface area	440,242,402 km^2
Mass	4.218 x 10^{24} kg
Volume	8.68584 x 10^{11} km^3
Mean density	4.856 g/cm^3
Surface gravity	0.71 g (Earth being 1 g)

Escape velocity	9.75 km/s
Equatorial rotation velocity	221.208 m/s
Surface temperature	178.7 K (minimum)
	297.5 K (mean)
	336.4 K (maximum)
Atmospheric pressure	124.6 kPa
Atmospheric composition	66.45% Nitrogen
	31.32% Oxygen
	0.07% Carbon dioxide
	1.16% Argon
	1.00% Water vapor

DUSKPEDIA

After reading this novella, you might wish to know more about some of the content addressed in this story. Here they are:

<u>Weapons used in this novella</u>

▶ FT-34 Freezethrower

- Affiliation: Hexiron
- Throws ice cold flames
- Designed to freeze targets and extinguish all categories of fires
- Ammunition: Freezethrower canisters

▶ P89 Slicer minelayer

- Affiliation: Hexiron
- Fires specially designed mines
- When nearby movement has been detected, the mines will jump vertically into the air and detonate
- Upon detonation, the mine unleashes plasma rings of blades horizontally in all directions
- Also designed to render tracked or wheeled vehicles immobile by slicing their tracks or wheels off
- Loads slicing mines from an external ammunition storage through a built-in portal
- Ammunition: Slicing mines

► S84 Shatterer submachine gun

- Affiliation: Hexiron
- The standard submachine gun of Hexiron
- Rate of fire: 800 rounds per minute
- Ammunition size: 5.56 mm
- Compatible ammunition types: Standard rounds, danium shards and rail rounds

► M777 Wingman assault rifle

- Affiliation: Hexiron
- The more sophisticated variant of the assault rifles of Hexiron
- Includes a M777 Archer device that fires manually when all magazines has been depleted of rounds
- Each M777 Archer includes two sharp ends at its front to provide additional penetration power
- When fired, the M777 Archer travels at a speed of 100 m/s
- Rate of fire: 500 rounds per minute
- Ammunition size: 5.56 mm
- Compatible ammunition types: Standard rounds, danium shards and rail rounds

► M792 Hunter assault rifle

- The more sophisticated variant of the assault rifles of Hexiron
- Most commonly used among supersoldiers of Hexiron
- Rate of fire: 800 rounds per minute
- Ammunition size: 5.56 mm
- Compatible ammunition types: Standard rounds, danium shards and rail rounds

▶ H17 Hadal Rifle (plasma repeater)

- Affiliation: Scentellian Federation
- Fires superheated violet-colored plasma bolts
- Continuous firing heats the weapon up and slows its rate of fire down
- Cools by ventilating
- Maximum rate of fire: 900 rounds per minute
- Ammunition type: Energy cells

▶ RP3 rocket pistol

- Affiliation: Hexiron
- A specially designed pistol that fires high explosive chronium-propelled rockets, which are to be manually loaded
- The rockets leave behind cyan-colored propulsion trails
- Upon detonation, a cyan-colored explosion will result
- The rocket has an arming distance of 40 metres, meaning that it will not detonate unless it has travelled more than this distance after being fired
- Chronium is a fictional cyan-colored and luminous fluid that burns to produce cyan-colored flames, thereby providing propulsion
- Each rocket from the RP3 rocket pistol has the explosive power equivalent to an explosion from the warhead of a MATADOR rocket launcher

▶ M173 Needle sniper rifle

- Affiliation: Hexiron
- The standard sniper rifle of Hexiron
- Number of rounds per magazine: 5
- Compatible ammunition types: Standard rounds, danium shards and rail rounds

- You can view its full 3D model at the 3D Warehouse at https://3dwarehouse.sketchup.com/model.html?id=708647ee cc904d7c75ff301d2cc50f1 (or simply visit the 3D warehouse and type the name of the weapon into the search box)

▶ The Danium Sword

- Affiliation: Hexiron
- A specially designed sword that is completely made of danium, which is a diamond-like teal-colored and transparent material
- The sword is equipped with corrosive edges that lights up when activated
- You can view its full 3D model at the 3D Warehouse at https://3dwarehouse.sketchup.com/model.html?id=78d dd06829ab8e30fadbdbbffadb05d5 (or simply visit the 3D warehouse and type the name of the weapon into the search box)

Which is your most favorite weapon?

The PDAs of Hexiron

The PDAs of Hexiron are specially designed holographic projecting smartphones that can be installed or downloaded with a vast array of special, unique, and even bizarre applications, which can only be purchased from the online market of Hexiron via the "Market" application by its members.

Furthermore, they also recharge by themselves all the time, implying that they can still last without chargers. This is achieved with the help of built-in portal devices within them, which links them to external power sources, such as chronium power plants and space stations. However, continuous usage to watch videos or view the social media will still drain their batteries due to their low rate of charging.

If they are connected to chargers, their charging rate will be increased by three to five folds, so fast that they can be charged from 0% to 100% in just under 20 minutes.

Chronium should not be confused with the element chromium used in modern chemistry today. Note the difference of only one letter in their spellings. Chronium is a cyan-colored element that can only be found on chthonian planets in the Milky Way Galaxy. They are commonly extracted from rocks, and burnt to power ships, gadgets, vehicles, and many other things within the space cooperation.

PDA applications used in this novella

Black triangular arrows indicate PDA applications, while black dots indicate options selectable within them.

▶ The "Contacts" application

Stores a list of contacts of the user

▶ The "Morphology" application

Turns the user or a target into a scanned organism for some time

▶ The "Consciousness" application

- The "Hijacker" option
  Hijacks the conscious mind of a target with the user's mind for some time

- The "Swapper" option
  Swaps the consciousness of the user with a target for some time

- The "Vegetator" option
  Renders a target into a vegetative state by removing its consciousness for some time

▶ **The "Stasis" application**

- The "Speed up" option
  Creates a transparent and membranous plasma sphere where the time passing rate inside is substantially faster than the time passing rate outside. Keegan used this option in chapter 6

- The "Slow down" option
  Creates a transparent and membranous plasma sphere where the time passing rate inside is substantially slower than the time passing rate outside

▶ **The "Portal" application**

- The "Urinal" option
  Opens a portal on the interface of the PDA that leads to a toilet bowl

- The "PTP" (PDA to PDA) option
  Opens a portal on the interface of the PDA that links to another PDA

- The "WTW" (Wall to wall) option
  Opens two portals on targeted flat surfaces at separate locations

- The "Waste disposal" option
  Opens a portal on the interface of the PDA that leads to a waste disposal site

▶ The "Waterer" application

- Shoots a small stream of water from the tip of the PDA by using stored data of water from the "Storage" application

▶ The "Shrinker" application

- The "Whole" option
  Shrinks a target wholly

- The "Head only" option
  Only shrinks the head or the anterior reg ion of a target

▶ The "Inferno" application

- The "Ignite" option
  Sets a targeted area on fire

▶ The "Momentum reducer" application

- The "Reduce momentum" option
  Reduces the speed of a moving target

▶ The "Local radar" application

  Displays a map around the user (enemies or potential threats are shown as prominent red dots)

▶ The "Storage" application

  Stores physical objects in the PDA as data, and vice versa

▶ The "Time turner" application

- The "Select/deploy spawning point" option (this option is optional and was not used by Dusk in chapter 13)

Deploys spawning points after going back in time for future use

- The "Morph into creature after turning time" option Combines the "Morphology" application with this application to turn the user into a selected creature or form immediately after turning time

► The "Healer" application

Transfers stored data into living tissues to heal a wound or restore a broken bone

Which is your most favorite PDA application or option?

Application: _____

Option: _____

<u>Creatures that appeared in this novella</u>

► Pear-shaped plant creatures

- Comes in all sorts of shapes and sizes
- Dormant and absorbs nutrients from the ground when undisturbed, but becomes mobile and carnivorous when provoked

► Other plant creatures

- Comes in all sorts of forms, shapes, and sizes, such as vines and epiphytes
- Dormant and absorbs nutrients from the ground when undisturbed, but becomes mobile and carnivorous when provoked

- Extremely dangerous to humans

▶ Fire-breathing wyvern

- Dusk's pet dragon

- Named Sparkie

▶ Gigantic tarantula

- Extremely massive and dangerous

▶ Double-headed cobra without a rattle

▶ Fist-sized purple ants

- Very large ants that delivers excruciating pain to a victim when bitten

▶ Roc

- Gigantic eagle-like bird
- Able to lift a small elephant with its claws

▶ Blue phoenix

- Dusk's pet phoenix

▶ Six-legged reptilian goats

- Awkward-looking harmless creatures

▶ Sea hydras

- Triple headed underwater beasts
- Extremely massive

Which is your most favorite creature?

_____

Additional information not covered in this novella

Other than the weapons addressed in this novella, there are also other weapons not used in the weapons compartment of the *Heron* and the rescue dropship. Here they are:

1) The M714 A92 Spirit assault rifle of Hexiron

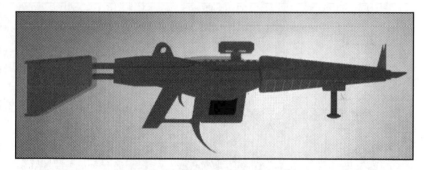

Being the much more advanced variant of the M4 carbine, The M714 A92 Spirit assault rifle is the standard assault rifle of Hexiron, as well as the most commonly used weapon by infantries in the military sector of the space cooperation. It can be loaded with multiple types of ammunition, which are standard 5.56 mm rounds, rail rounds and danium shards (diamond bullets).

You can view its full 3D model at the 3D Warehouse at https://3dwarehouse.sketchup.com/model.html?id=64bebec803a73 4fdc94a3d0e7fa449d7 (or simply visit the 3D warehouse and type the name of the weapon into the search box)

2) The SQ58 Blaster shotgun of Hexiron

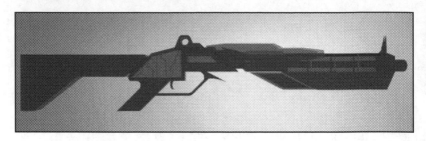

The SQ58 Blaster shotgun is the standard shotgun used in the military sector of Hexiron. Similar to the Spirit assault rifle, it can also be loaded with multiple types of ammunition, which are standard 5.56 mm shells, rail shells and danium shells (diamond ball bearings).

3) The MGR53 Thunder Gatling rifle of Hexiron

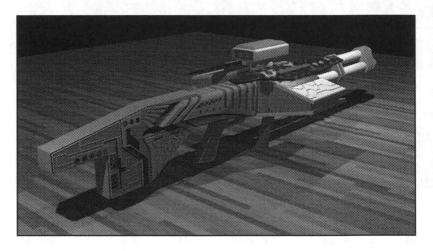

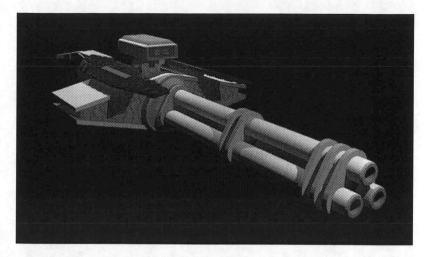

Similar in design to a small minigun, the MGR53 Thunder Gatling rifle is one of the heaviest and most powerful suppressive weapons in the military sector of Hexiron. Because of its immense weight, this weapon is always either carried by supersoldiers or mounted on a stand. Notice that Keegan took the freezethrower instead of this weapon because of this reason.

The weapon loads with 7.62 mm rounds of standard bullets, rail rounds or danium rounds (diamond bullets), and has a high rate of fire of 2,500 rounds per minute. It can also be attached with multiple weapon attachments, such as the rectangular-shaped device at the top of the weapon in the above images, which is known as the JI-72 digital scope, while the two danium plates at its sides function as forcefield generators.

Last but not least, the shoot that holds the bullets of this weapon is situated within its diamond-shaped metal compartment, and comes from a built-in portal device that links to an ammunition facility on another planet. This eliminates the hassle of transporting shoots, ammunition crates or boxes along with the weapon to battle.

You can view its full 3D model at the 3D Warehouse at https://3dwarehouse.sketchup.com/model.html?id=de0f9c9b67c5f 5a6422f205de59ac7e6 (or simply visit the 3D warehouse and type the name of the weapon into the search box)

4) Razor River

The Razor River is a fast-flowing river that flows down from three peaks on Droughalis, namely Mt Creep, Mt Crimp and Mt Creiol. The creatures inhabiting along this river include fast-moving snails that can move faster than the usual walking speed of humans, ravenous piranhas, carnivorous mangrove plants with poisonous roots and snake-like burrowing creatures that catches their prey by abruptly smashing up from the soil and pulling them down. Some of the trees near this river even have gigantic eyeballs in their trunks, which are used to observe and trap their prey with its vines and absorb nutrients from them.

5) Jrozi Reservoir

Jrozi reservoir is a massive water body found on the northwest of the island of Droughalis. Hydras and piranhas are the main predators inhabiting within this water body. Other inhabitants include floaters, which are plants that float and move on the water with balloon-like inflated membranes. They do not absorb water to grow, but consume fishes and other small aquatic creatures by grabbing them with their roots and pulling them to their mouths, which are all submerged underwater.

6) Hudi Island

Hudi Island is an offshore island situated to the north of Droughalis. It was once part of the main island, but was broken off due to prolonged exposure to strong wave currents and consistent soil erosion. The creatures inhabiting here is the same as that experienced by Dusk, Keegan and Raven on the main island.

THEME SONG

The theme song of this novella has been composed and recorded on piano. It can be found at http://www.youtube.com/watch?v=7VjUKYL43Y4

Alternatively, you can visit YouTube and type "Dusk: Death Island" into the search box to gain access to the soundtrack. Enjoy!

Of course, there are also many other soundtracks included in this novella, but was not considered for publication because I do not take music courses, and therefore lack the experience to produce complex orchestral pieces, which can only be achieved by a band of skilled musicians.

END